BY MIKHAIL BULGAKOV

THE MASTER AND MARGARITA

BLACK SNOW

A THEATRICAL NOVEL BY

MIKHAIL BULGAKOV

TRANSLATED FROM THE RUSSIAN BY MICHAEL GLENNY

SIMON AND SCHUSTER   NEW YORK

ABOUT MIKHAIL BULGAKOV, HIS NOVEL, THE MOSCOW ART THEATER, STANISLAVSKI

MIKHAIL BULGAKOV was born in 1891 and died on March 10th, 1940. *Black Snow: A Theatrical Novel* had to wait at least thirty years for publication before appearing in the August 1965 issue of the literary monthly *Novy Mir* under the title *A Theatrical Novel*. Until then Bulgakov's reputation in the Soviet Union was based largely on his plays. He is said to have written thirty-six plays, of which eleven were published and eight performed. Although in his early days Bulgakov wrote a number of short stories, some were never published at all, some sank without trace along with the ephemeral journals that had printed them, some were only printed abroad by emigré publishers and none of the few that appeared in Russia ever came out in big editions or achieved republication.

The work which brought Bulgakov virtually overnight success was his play *The Days of the Turbins*, a dramatized version of his own novel *The White Guard*. The theme of both novel and play was the bitter Civil War which raged in Russia for nearly three years after the Bolshevik revolution, fought between the "Whites"—an imprecise generalization covering many shades of political opposition to Bolshevism—and the "Reds." Like all civil wars it was peculiarly savage: the trauma which split and scarred the Russian nation was really the Civil War and its aftermath of chaos and famine rather than the relatively bloodless revolution. This terrible period formed the subject matter of countless stories, novels, poems, plays and films. With one or two outstanding exceptions they all, rather naturally, depicted the Civil War either entirely from the Red viewpoint or in complete sympathy with the Reds.

The most startling fact about Bulgakov's novel-turned-play was that it showed the Civil War wholly from the side of the Whites. This may not strike us as very startling, but it was an extraordinarily daring thing to do in the Soviet Russia of the twenties where the wounds of the struggle had not yet healed and where the government was acutely sensitive to the open conspiracy among White Russian emigrés to discredit and if possible to subvert the Bolshevik regime. What was more, *The Days of the Turbins* implicitly rejected the official Communist Party attitude to the opposing sides in the Civil War by refusing to depict the Whites as bloodthirsty reactionaries or as evil buffoons of unrelieved villainy and instead showing them as ordinary, honest, rather bewildered people who reacted with human predictability to the collapse of the world as they had known it.

Yet such was the compelling skill and dramatic power of *The Days of the Turbins* that it not only survived the Party's initial disapproval of its political message but remained as one of the best-loved and most successful plays of the Soviet theater's entire repertoire. . . . First staged by the Moscow Art Theater in 1926, it was an immediate and resounding success with the public. Three years later the theater censor had it banned, but in 1932 Bulgakov made a personal appeal to Stalin to have the ban removed. Stalin asked to see it again. After four frantic days of preparation (the play was then of course out of repertory: the sets and costumes had to be hauled out of storage, the cast reassembled and rehearsed) the Moscow Art Theater put on a special performance for Stalin alone and with a few minor alterations the ruler of Soviet Russia allowed it back onto the stage.

It remained in regular production at the M.A.T. (running for a total of nine hundred and eighty-seven performances) until 1941, when all the sets were destroyed that summer in a German air raid on Minsk. The M.A.T. never staged it again, but in 1954 Mikhail Yanshin, who had played one of the leading parts in the original cast, revived it at the Stanislavski Theater in Moscow where it is still being performed to this day, in a production substantially the same as Stanislavski's. Among its many productions outside Russia, *The Days of the Turbins*—under the original title of the novel, *The White Guard*—ran in London at the Phoenix Theater in 1938, directed by Michael Saint Denis in Rodney Acland's translation. More recently Rudolph Cartier produced it on B.B.C. Television in 1960, with Marius Goring in the star part of Alexei Turbin. Besides Acland's version it is also available in English, translated by F. D. Reeve, in Vol. II of the paperback *Anthology of Russian Plays* (Vintage Books, New York, 1963). The play has been translated into many other languages.

Black Snow is Bulgakov's own story, under a thin but intriguing veil of fiction, of how he came to write *The White Guard* and to recast it as the play *The Days of the Turbins*. None of the very few people who have studied Bulgakov's career have so far been able to state when *Black Snow* was written. For the present this information is probably known only to the author's widow, who owns all his papers and manuscripts, and to the scholars who comprise the Commission set up to act as Bulgakov's literary executors.

I incline to think that it was written in the last few years of his life, between 1936 and 1939. Despite setbacks and the rapid onset of ill-health, these years were an extraordinarily productive finale to Bulgakov's career. *Black Snow*, because it is unfinished, was probably one of his very last works. Bulgakov went blind in September 1939 and died seven months later.

It could be thought pedantic to set out to comment on such a witty book as this since much of the charm of *Black Snow*, with its mocking, self-deprecating view of literary and theatrical Moscow in the midtwenties, lies in its lightness of touch. At the risk of smothering the novel in exegesis, however, the reader's pleasure may perhaps be increased in some degree by being given the key to the main events and characters. The Russian reading public will have delightedly recognized most of the real persons in Bulgakov's mischievous and often savage caricatures, so it is only fair to let English-speaking readers in on the joke.

To begin at the beginning, the "Independent Theater" is of course the Moscow Art Theater, with which Bulgakov was intimately connected for the ten years beginning in 1925 when his play was commissioned, first as an author, later as one of the staff: from 1930 to 1935 he held the jobs of assistant producer and "dramaturg" or resident playwright. Although he loved the theater and the Moscow Art in particular Bulgakov was temperamentally incapable of the total, uncritical devotion which the M.A.T. demanded from the members of the company; with his great intelligence, his integrity and the natural reserve of his manner he remained "with" the M.A.T. but not "of" it. Knowing the place inside out yet always slightly detached, his stance was that of a clever, disillusioned and sarcastic friend who spared no one when it came to ridiculing vanity, insincerity and bitchiness. A few, however, of the Moscow Art staff earned Bulgakov's respect and devoted friendship, among them Pavel Alexandrovich Markov, who appears in *Black Snow* as "Misha Panin" the literary editor, the job that Markov held at the real-life M.A.T. Markov was the man who spotted Bulgakov's novel *The White Guard* when it appeared in serial form in a literary monthly and it was he who helped and advised

Bulgakov in the difficult work of adapting it for the stage. It was one of Markov's first and most successful "discoveries" of a new playwriting talent: he had just started his job as literary editor in 1925, the year in which the action of the story begins. Bulgakov remained his friend for the rest of his life and showed his gratitude by the affectionate way he characterized "Panin" in a cast largely made up of fools or knaves.

The prelude to the main or "theatrical" part of the book is the "literary" episode surrounding the writing and publication of *Black Snow* as a novel. Allowing for comic exaggeration and a coating of the grotesque, it corresponds to what must have been a restless and unhappy period of Bulgakov's life. His mother, to whom he had been deeply attached, had died in 1922. Like his hero "Maxudov" in *Black Snow*, Bulgakov worked as a journalist and hated it. The incongruous-sounding title of the *Shipping Gazette* is a disguise for the magazine where he worked as a staff reporter and feature writer: its real name was *The Whistle* (in Russian *Gudok*), so-called because it was the journal of the Railwaymen's Union. This remarkable publication was no mere trade union house organ: it had an amazingly high literary standard and was a nursery of writing talent. The actual name of the literary monthly to which Bulgakov gives the fictitious title of *The Motherland* was *Russia* (in Russian *Rossiya*) and the real-life equivalent of its Mephistophelean editor "Rudolfi" was a man called J. G. Lezhnev. In the fictional version, "Maxudov" is made out to be much more obscure and unsuccessful than Bulgakov himself really was at the time: he had already been published in several annuals and magazines, including *Russia* itself, as a result of which he had established a genuine if modest reputation as a writer of humorous short stories. On the back cover of the July 1924 issue of *Russia* there is an announcement of forthcoming works to be published which lists Bulgakov's name along with other star contributors, who include Boris Pasternak and Ilya Ehrenburg. There is no doubt, though, that it was the serial publication in the April and May 1925 issues of *Russia* of *The White Guard* which was the crucial turning-point in Bulgakov's career and it is for this reason that he built up the parallel episode in *Black Snow* to such heights of tragicomic drama, complete with Maxudov's bungled attempt at suicide. Like its fictional counterpart, the magazine *Russia* folded up after only publishing two installments of Bulgakov's novel.

All this, however, is a mere overture to the main theme of Bulgakov's deeply felt love-hate relationship with the Moscow Art Theater and its two codirectors. One half of the duumvirate which had ruled the M.A.T. since its foundation in 1897 was Vladimir Ivanovich Nemirovich-Danchenko; in *Black Snow* Bulgakov calls him "Aristarkh Platonovich." This purposely somewhat un-Russian name, with its Hellenic associations, is Bulgakov's way of poking fun at the rather precious manners of classical estheticism cultivated by the upper strata of the Russian intelligentsia.

It is the better-known one of this pair of theatrical autocrats who is the target for the full force of Bulgakov's withering satire. It can hardly be necessary to reveal that the character masquerading under the name and patronymic of "Ivan Vasilievich" is Konstantin Sergeyevich Stanislavski. Our shock on recognizing his lineaments in this savage caricature is all the greater because it has been the general custom, in Russia as everywhere else, to describe Stanislavski in terms of unadulterated respect and admiration. Far from being captivated by the great man's legendary charm and theatrical genius, Bulgakov depicts him as a vain, tyrannical old bitch. Although prepared to acknowledge his talent as an actor, he remorselessly tears every other element of Stanislavski's reputation to shreds until we are left with an emperor who is naked—except to his fawning court. His charm is revealed as no more than a tool with which to manipulate people, his dedication is unmasked as the purest egomania, his fostering of artistic talent as sheer favoritism; his famous "method" has ossified into a set of idiosyncratic mannerisms deeply inimical to any spark of original talent. The harmony and unity which outwardly characterized the Moscow Art Theater company is debunked as largely a sham. Riven vertically between the Stanislavski devotees on one side and the protégés of Nemirovich-Danchenko on the other, there is an equally yawning horizontal gulf between the aspiring younger generation of actors and the old stagers who are fiercely determined to go on hogging all the good parts. As Bulgakov adds stroke after merciless stroke to his picture of backstage life, it becomes a matter of some wonder that this menagerie of inflated egos actually managed to stage a performance every night. It is of course a caricature and not a photograph, but like all great ironists he exaggerates and distorts for a purpose. The rarefied, enclosed world of the M.A.T., with its jealousies, feuds and temperamental showing-off was a natural and legitimate target for a writer of such brilliant satirical talent.

Yet the fact is that the main episode which *Black Snow* ostensibly describes—the dramatization and staging of Bulgakov's novel *The White Guard*—was not the exasperating farce that he implies. He got on well with the play's producer, Ilya Sudakov (who appears in *Black Snow* as "Thomas Strizh") and although his attitude stopped short of idolatry, he was also on excellent terms with Stanislavski and remained so for several years. Bulgakov's disillusionment with Stanislavski, which is of that intensity peculiar to soured and rejected love, dates from an event that took place ten years after the successful production of his first play.

In 1932 Bulgakov wrote a tragedy entitled *Molière*. It records with great poignancy the last months of Molière's life when the great actor-playwright, after a life of exhausting struggle finally crowned with success, was harried to death by a clique of jealous hypocrites surrounding Louis XIV. The parallel with Bulgakov's own treatment by Stalin's censorship (it was written at a time when all his plays and short stories had been banned) was intentional and evident to anybody who could read between the lines. Stanislavski, who for political reasons badly needed a new play by a Soviet author, accepted the play and intended to produce it, but he was ill when rehearsals were due to begin and handed over the job to another Moscow Art producer, N. M. Gorchakov. Work on the play lasted four years and turned out to be an extremely unhappy experience for all concerned. In an attempt to disguise its thinly concealed attack on the Communist Party, Gorchakov turned the play into a conventional period melodrama. This infuriated Bulgakov, who flatly rejected Stanislavski's repeated demands to rewrite large parts of the play. Rehearsals dragged on in an exhausting succession of rows and sulks. At long last came the première in February 1936, with Bulgakov still fuming and Stanislavski prostrate with anxiety and frustration. The Party-controlled press understood the play's intention only too well and after a chorus of blistering reviews *Molière* was taken off after a run of only seven nights. The whole affair had shattered Stanislavski and embittered Bulgakov, who resigned his post at the M.A.T. in a cold rage.

With its subject-matter antedated by ten years to his début as a playwright, *Black Snow: A Theatrical Novel* is Bulgakov's revenge on Stanislavski for the failure of *Molière*.

M.G.

PART ONE

CHAPTER ONE

HOW IT ALL BEGAN

ON APRIL 29th Moscow was washed clean by a thunderstorm. The air was delightful; it mellowed the heart and made one want to start living again. In my new gray suit and a fairly respectable overcoat I set off walking along one of the main streets of the capital to an unfamiliar address. The reason for my journey was an unexpected letter, which was in my pocket. It read:

DEAR SERGEI LEONTIEVICH,

I should very much like to meet you and have a talk with you about a highly confidential matter which may be of the greatest interest to you. If you are free, please come to the Academy of Drama attached to the Independent Theater on Wednesday at four o'clock.

Yours,

X. ILCHIN

The letter was written on paper headed in the top left-hand corner as follows:

Xavier Borisovich Ilchin, Producer
Academy of Drama
The Independent Theater

Although this was the first time that I had ever seen Ilchin's name, I had heard of the Academy of Drama. I had also heard of the Independent Theater and knew that it was one of the best theaters, but I had never been inside it. The letter had excited me, particularly as I was getting no letters at all at the time. I should mention that I was a junior on the *Shipping Gazette*. I was living in a horrible little room— though at least I had it to myself—on the seventh floor in the Krasniye Vorota district, in a cul-de-sac called Khomutovsky Street.

Well, there I was, walking along breathing in the freshened air, and wondering whether the thunderstorm would strike again, wondering too how on earth Xavier Ilchin had learned of my existence, how he had found where I lived and what business he might have that concerned me; but rack my brain as I might, I had no idea what this could possibly be and finally I decided that Ilchin must want to exchange rooms with me. Of course I should have written to Ilchin telling him to come and see me since he had something to discuss with me, but I confess I was ashamed of my room and ashamed of my neighbors. I am a rather odd person and somewhat afraid of people in general. Imagine Ilchin coming in and seeing my couch with its cover torn and a spring sticking out, my table lamp with its shade made out of newspaper, a cat walking about and the sound of Annushka swearing from the kitchen.

I passed through some wrought-iron gates, noticing a little booth where a gray-haired man sat selling badges and eyeglass frames. I jumped over a muddy stream of rainwater and found myself in front of a yellow painted building and the thought occurred to me that it had been built long, long ago, before either Ilchin or I had been born. A black plaque lettered in gold announced it as the Academy of Drama. I went in; a short man with a little beard, wearing a tunic with green lapels, immediately barred my way.

"Who do you want to see, citizen?" he asked suspiciously, spreading out his hands as if he were trying to catch a hen.

"I have to see Ilchin, the producer," I said, trying to sound arrogant. The man changed visibly. His hands dropped to the seams of his trousers and he smiled a fawning smile.

"Xavier Borisovich? At once, sir. Please take off your coat, sir. Have you no galoshes?" The man took my coat as reverently as if it had been a precious ecclesiastical vestment. I walked up an iron staircase, noticing the bas-reliefs depicting helmeted warriors brandishing swords, old-fashioned Dutch stoves with hot-air vents that had been polished until they shone like gold. The building was silent, there was not a soul anywhere except the green-lapeled man plodding up behind me and when I turned around I saw that he was making me a whole series of wordless signs indicating respect, devotion, servility, love, delight that I had come and assurance that although he was walking behind me he was guiding me, leading me to the abode of the lonely, enigmatic Xavier Borisovich Ilchin.

Suddenly it grew dark, the Dutch stoves lost their oily, whitish gleam and the murk at once closed in. Outside, the second thunderstorm burst.

I knocked on a door, went in and in the gloom I at last saw Xavier Borisovich.

"My name is Maxudov," I said with dignity.

Somewhere far away over Moscow lightning split the sky, illuminating Ilchin in a momentary phosphorescent flash.

"So there you are, my dear Sergei Leontievich!" said Ilchin, with a crafty smile. And then Ilchin led me, grasping me around the waist, to exactly the same couch that I had in my room; even the spring was sticking out in the same place where mine stuck out—in the middle.

To this day I don't know what that room was in which that fateful meeting took place. Why was that couch there? What were those sheets of music lying scattered in a corner? Why was there a pair of scales standing on the windowsill with teacups on it? Why did Ilchin meet me in that room and not, say, in the adjoining room where in the distance the vague outlines of a grand piano could be made out in the twilight of the storm?

In between the muttering of the thunder Xavier Borisovich said:

"I have read your novel."

I gave a start. You see . . .

CHAPTER TWO

THE ONSET
OF NEUROSIS

YOU SEE, working in the humble capacity of a proof-reader on the *Shipping Gazette*, I hated the job and at nights in my attic, sometimes until the light of dawn, I had written a novel.

It began one night when I woke up after a nightmare. I had been dreaming of my home town; snow, winter, the Civil War . . . In my dream a snowstorm whirled soundlessly before my eyes and then came a grand piano and people standing around it. I was oppressed by a terrible sense of loneliness in the dream; I felt deeply sorry for myself and woke up in tears. I turned on the light, a dusty little bulb which lit up my poverty: a cheap and nasty little inkwell, a few books, a pile of old newspapers. My left side was aching from the broken spring, fear gripped my heart. I felt that at any minute I was going to die. This terrible fear of death weighed on me with such force that I groaned aloud and looked around in alarm in search of some prop, some defense against death. And I found it. The cat, which I had put out of doors earlier, was meowing. The animal was alarmed. In a second it was sitting on my newspapers, looking at me with round eyes and asking: what has happened? This skinny, smoke-gray cat was concerned about me. Who would feed my old cat if I were to die?

"It's the onset of neurosis," I explained to the cat; "it will get worse and engulf me. But I shan't die just yet." The house was asleep. I looked out of the window. There was no light on any of the five stories and I saw it not as a house but as a ship with many decks, gliding along under a motionless black sky. The idea that we were moving cheered me up. I calmed down, the cat calmed down too and shut its eyes.

That was how I started writing my novel. I described the snowstorm from my dream. I tried to describe how the side of the grand piano shone in the light of a shaded lamp. It did not work out, but I persevered. In the daytime I had a single aim—to expend as little as possible of my strength on the job that I so detested. I worked mechanically so as not to exert my brain. At every suitable opportunity I went absent from work on the pretext of being ill. No one believed me, of course, and life became unpleasant but I stuck it out and gradually got used to it. I waited for the night with all the impatience of a young man waiting for his beloved. Only then was it quiet enough in my accursed room. I sat down at the table. The cat liked sitting on the newspapers, but it was even more interested in my novel and it would watch for the right moment to move over from a sheet of newspaper onto a sheet of manuscript. I would then pick it up by the scruff of its neck and put it back in its place.

One night I raised my head in amazement. My ship was sailing nowhere, the house was standing still and it was broad daylight. My lamp was unnecessary, its light irritating and unpleasant. I switched it off and my loathsome room stood before me in the light of dawn. Cats of various hues were silently, furtively padding about across the asphalted courtyard. Every letter on my page could be read without the help of the lamp. "My God! It's April!" I exclaimed. In bold letters I wrote: "The End." The end of winter, the end of blizzards, the end of the cold. During the winter I had lost my few acquaintances and had shut myself off; I had caught rheumatism and grown somewhat unsociable. But I had shaved every day. With all this in my mind I put the cat out-of-doors then returned and went to sleep. For the first time since winter I slept without dreaming. The novel needed a lot of correcting. Countless passages had to be crossed out, hundreds of words changed. It would be a long but essential job. Unfortunately I was tempted to neglect it and having corrected only the first six pages I returned to the world of people. I invited some guests. They included two men from the *Shipping Gazette*—working journalists like myself—their wives and two writers. One was a young man who had surprised me by the way he wrote short stories with such inimitable skill and the other was an elderly man of the world who turned out on closer acquaintance to be the most appalling swine.

In that one evening I read aloud approximately a quarter of my novel. The wives were so bored by my reading that I felt some pangs of conscience, but the journalists and writers were tougher. Their opinions were as sincere as if we had been brothers, pretty harsh and, as I now realize, justified.

"The language!" cried one of the writers (the one who turned out to be such a swine). "The language is the trouble. It's no good." He drank a large glass of vodka and swallowed a sardine. I poured him out another glass. He drank it and ate a piece of sausage.

"Metaphors!" he shouted, munching.

"Yes," the young writer agreed, "the language is a bit weak."

The journalists said nothing but nodded sympathetically and drank. The ladies didn't even nod, said nothing, refused the port specially bought for them and drank vodka. "How can you expect it to be anything but weak," shouted the elderly man, "good writing won't just come when you whistle, I'd have you know. Unless you've got it, you haven't a hope. Not a hope. Remember that, old man!" The "old man" was obviously aimed at me. I froze.

As they left they agreed to come and see me again and a week later they returned. I read the second part. The evening was marked by the elderly litterateur treating me in a way which I thought maudlin and overfamiliar. He started calling me "Leontich."

"The language is hopeless! But it's intriguing. God damn you (me!) it's intriguing!" the elderly man shouted as he demolished one of Dusya's jellies.

On the third evening a new man appeared, also a writer, with an evil Mephistophelian face, a cast in his left eye and unshaven. He said the novel was bad, but he would like to hear the fourth and last part. A woman who had just been divorced came too and a man with a guitar in a case. I learned a lot by giving that party. My shy colleagues from the *Gazette* thawed out slightly and expressed their opinions. One said that chapter seventeen was too long, the other that the character of Vasienka was not sufficiently rounded out. Both of them were right. The fourth and last reading was not held in my room, but in the apartment of the young man who was so clever at writing short stories. This time about twenty people turned up and I met the young writer's grandmother, a charming old lady, spoiled by only one characteristic—a look of terror which never left her all evening. Apart from her there was their old nanny, asleep on a chest. I finished the novel. Disaster. They all said as one man that my novel was unprintable because it would never be passed by the censorship. Only then did I realize that while I had been writing the novel it had never occurred to me whether it might pass the censorship or not. One of the women began it by saying (I later discovered that she too had been divorced), "Tell me, Maxudov, do you think your novel will get past the censor?"

"Never, never, never," cried the elderly writer; "never,

under any circumstances. There's no question of it being passed! Simply no hope of it. Don't worry, old man—they'll never pass it."

"They won't pass it!" chorused the people around the end of the table.

"The language . . ." the guitarist's brother began to say, but the elderly man interrupted him.

"To hell with the language," he shouted, heaping salad onto his plate. "The language is not the point. The old chap writes badly, but it's an intriguing novel. You're observant all right, you rascal; don't know where you get it from, never suspected it was in you—but the story! . . ."

"Mm, yes, the story . . ."

"Exactly—the story," shouted the elderly man and woke up the old nanny, "you know what's needed . . . You don't know? Aha! Well, now!"

He winked, drinking as he did so. Then he embraced me and kissed me, shouting:

"There's something nasty about you, you know. There is, believe me. But I like you. I like you, strike me dead on the spot if I'm lying. He's cunning, this rogue, he's a devious, cunning man. Isn't he? Did you listen carefully to chapter four? Did you hear what he said to the heroine? I mean to say! . . ."

"Firstly, what do you mean . . ." I was about to begin, infuriated by his familiarity.

"First you must kiss me," shouted the elderly writer. "Don't you want to? Anyone can see what sort of a chap you are. No, my friend, you're not the simple, honest sort of person I thought you were!"

"He's obviously not at all simple," echoed the other divorcé.

"Firstly . . ." I began again angrily, but got no further.

"Firstly nothing!" shouted the elderly man. "You're a bit of a Dostoevski, aren't you! Yes, you are. All right, you don't like me. God forgive you for it, I don't mind. But we all sincerely like you and wish you nothing but good." Here he pointed to the guitarist's brother and another total stranger with a purple face, who on arriving had apologized for being late, saying that he had been at the public baths. "And I'm telling you straight," went on the elderly man, "because I'm used to telling the truth to people's faces—you, Leontich, will never get anywhere with this novel. You'll have nothing but trouble and we, your friends, will go through hell at the thought of it! Believe me! I'm a man of enormous and bitter experience; I know life. Go on," he shouted, gesturing to everybody to be his witnesses, "go on, look at me, stare at me like a wild beast if you like! There's gratitude for being so decent to you! Leontich!"—he gave such a scream that the old nanny behind her little curtain got up from the chest—"you'd better realize, my lad, that this novel of yours is not such a great work of art . . . (at this point a soft chord on the guitar was heard from the sofa) . . . that you need go and crucify yourself. I'm telling you!"

"He's telling you, telling you, telling you . . ." the guitarist began singing in a pleasing tenor.

"And this is what I say," shouted the elderly man, "I say that if you don't kiss me at once then I'm going to get up and leave this delightful party—because you have insulted me!"

Suffering inexpressibly, I kissed him. By this time a chorus was well under way and the tenor sang unctuously and tenderly above it, "Telling you, telling you . . ."

Like a cat I crept furtively out of the apartment, clutching the heavy manuscript under my arm. The old nanny, with reddened, tear-stained eyes, was bending and drinking water from the kitchen tap. Without knowing why, I handed her a ruble.

"Get away with you," said the nanny angrily, brushing aside my ruble "Four o'clock in the morning! It's like the tortures of the damned!"

In the distance a familiar voice boomed over the chorus, "Where is he? Run away? Stop him! What did I tell you, comrades! . . ."

But the oilcloth-lined door had already let me out and I fled without looking around.

CHAPTER THREE

I COMMIT SUICIDE

"G o d, it was awful," I said to myself in my room, "every-thing was awful. The salad, the nanny, the elderly writer, that unforgettable 'telling you,' my whole life is awful."

An autumn wind was moaning outside, there was a clatter-ing noise from a piece of torn corrugated iron, and sheets of rain were creeping across the windowpanes. After the party with the nanny and the guitar lots of things happened but all of them so unpleasant that I would rather not write about them. Firstly, I stopped checking my novel to see whether or not the censorship might pass it. It was obvious that they would not. The elderly man was quite right; every line of the novel seemed to shriek it. Having corrected the manuscript I spent my last remaining money on having two extracts type-written and sent to the editor of a literary journal. Two weeks later I got them back. In one corner of the typescript was written "Unsuitable."

After that my cat died. She had stopped eating, had huddled herself into a corner and meowed until I was driven into a frenzy. It lasted for three days and on the fourth I found her in the corner motionless on her back. I borrowed a shovel from the caretaker and buried the cat in the patch of wasteland behind our house. I was now totally alone in the world but I confess that in my heart of hearts I was glad. What a burden the wretched animal had been to me!

Then the rain came and my shoulder and left knee started aching; yet worst of all was the fact that my novel was no good. If it was bad, it meant the end of my life. Spend the rest of my life working on the *Gazette*? You're joking.

Every night I lay staring into the hellish darkness and repeating: "It's terrible." If someone had asked me what I remembered of the time I worked on the *Shipping Gazette*, I would have replied with a clear conscience—nothing. Muddy galoshes around the hatstand, someone's wet hat with long, pendulous ear flaps; nothing more. "It's terrible," I repeated, as I listened to the silence of the night roaring in my ears. After about two weeks I began to feel the effects of insomnia. I took a streetcar to Samotechnaya-Sadovaya Street where there lived, in a house whose number I shall of course keep a strict secret, a man whose job gave him the right to carry arms. How I got to know him does not matter. Entering his apartment I found my friend lying on the sofa. While he made tea on the primus in his kitchen, I opened the left-hand drawer of his writing desk and removed his Browning automatic; then I drank some tea and went home.

It was about nine o'clock in the evening. I arrived home. Everything was as it always was—a smell of roast mutton coming from the kitchen, the corridor full of the usual fog dimly pierced by an electric light which glowed from the ceiling. I went into my room. The light flashed from above and then the room was instantly plunged into darkness. The bulb had burned out.

"It's all part of a pattern; it is fate," I said grimly.

I lit the oil stove on the floor in the corner. On a sheet of paper I wrote: "I hereby declare that I have stolen from Parfyon Ivanovich (adding his surname, the number of his house and the street) a Browning automatic No. ——" (I forget the number). I signed it and laid it on the floor beside the oil stove. Mortal fear overcame me. It is a terrible thing to die. Then I imagined our corridor, the mutton, the elderly writer and the *Gazette* and cheered up at the thought of the noise they would make when they broke down my door. I put the muzzle to my temple and felt for the trigger with a shaky finger. At that moment I heard a familiar sound from downstairs, a squeaky orchestra struck up and a tenor began singing on a phonograph record, "But will not God return me all!"

"Heavens! *Faust!*" I thought. "How timely. I'll just wait for Mephistopheles' entry. For the last time. I shall never hear it again." The orchestra alternately rose and faded, but the tenor shrieked louder and louder, "I curse this life, my faith and all my knowledge!"

"In a moment," I thought, "but he's singing it so fast . . ."

The tenor gave a despairing yell, then the orchestra came in with a crash. My trembling finger lay on the trigger and for a moment the noise deafened me. My heart seemed to fail and the flame of the oil stove seemed to shoot up toward the ceiling; I dropped the revolver.

Then the noise came again. A ponderous bass voice rang out, "It is I!"

I turned toward the door.

CHAPTER FOUR

CLOAK AND SWORD

SOMEONE was knocking at the door, repeatedly and authoritatively. I stuck the revolver into my trousers pocket and cried weakly, "Come in."

The door was flung open and I collapsed to the floor with horror. It was him, without the slightest doubt. In the twilight there towered over me a face with an imperious nose and beetling eyebrows. The play of shadows made me see a pointed black beard jutting from his square chin. A beret was planted jauntily over one ear. It lacked feathers, it is true, but in a word the apparition before me was—Mephistopheles. Then I looked again and saw that he was wearing an overcoat and shiny blue galoshes. He was carrying a briefcase under his arm. "Of course, that's right," I thought, "how else would he walk around Moscow in the middle of the twentieth century?"

"Rudolfi," said the evil spirit in a tenor, not a bass voice. He need not have introduced himself. I recognized him. There in my room stood one of the most notable figures in the literary world of the time: Ilya Ivanovich Rudolfi, editor of the only privately owned magazine in Russia, *The Motherland*.

I got up from the floor.

"Why don't you put the light on?" asked Rudolfi.

"Unfortunately I can't," I replied, "because my bulb has burned out and I haven't got another one."

The evil spirit in the shape of the editor did one of his simpler tricks—he produced an electric light bulb out of his briefcase.

"Do you always carry bulbs about with you?" I asked in amazement.

"No," said the spirit sternly, "pure coincidence. I just happen to have been shopping."

When the room was lit and Rudolfi had taken off his overcoat, I furtively removed from the table the note with my confession of the theft of the revolver and the spirit pretended not to have noticed it.

We sat down. A short silence.

"Have you written a novel?" Rudolfi finally asked in a harsh voice.

"How do you know?"

"Likospastov told me."

"Well, you see . . ." I began (Likospastov was the elderly writer) "actually I . . . well . . . the fact is, it's a very bad novel."

"I see," said the spirit, staring intently at me. I then noticed that he had no beard after all. The shadows had fooled me.

"Show it to me," said Rudolfi masterfully.

"No, I won't," I replied.

"*Show it to me*," said Rudolfi emphasizing each word separately.

"They'll never pass it . . ."

"Show it to me."

"You see, it's written in manuscript and I have very bad handwriting. My O's come out like a single stroke and . . ."

At this point my hands were unconsciously opening the drawer which contained the wretched novel.

"I can read any handwriting as if it were print," explained Rudolfi. "It's part of my job." The manuscript was in his hands.

An hour passed. I sat by the oil stove heating up some water, while Rudolfi read the novel. A host of thoughts whirled in my head, chiefly about Rudolfi. He was a remarkable editor and it was considered an honor to appear in his magazine. I should have been delighted at his coming to see me, even in the guise of Mephistopheles. On the other hand he might not like my novel and that would be awkward . . . Apart from that I felt that my suicide, interrupted at the crucial point, was off; consequently I would be back again tomorrow in the depths of poverty. What is more I should have been offering him some tea and I had no sugar. My head was in a thorough muddle, made no better by the thought of having stolen the revolver to no purpose.

Meanwhile Rudolfi was devouring page after page and I tried in vain to discover what impression the novel was making on him. Rudolfi's face expressed precisely nothing at all.

When he paused to wipe his glasses, I added one more stupidity to the several I had already uttered, "What did Likospastov say about my novel?"

"He said your novel was hopeless," answered Rudolfi coldly and turned over a page. ("That swine Likospastov! Instead of backing up a friend . . ." and so on.)

At one A.M. we drank some tea and by two o'clock Rudolfi had read the whole novel. I was fidgeting on the sofa.

"Well," said Rudolfi.

Silence.

"Are you trying to imitate Tolstoi?" said Rudolfi.

"Which Tolstoi?" I asked. "There were several of them. Aleksei Konstantinovich the well-known writer, Pyotr Andreevich who went abroad and captured the Tsarevich Alexis,

the numismatist Ivan Ivanovich, or do you mean Leo Niko-
laevich?"

"Where did you study?"

Here I must reveal a little secret. The fact is that I gradu-
ated from two faculties at the university, but I would not
admit to it.

"I went to a church parish school," I said with a cough.

"Did you indeed," said Rudolfi, a faint smile touching
his lips. Then he asked: "How many times a week do you
shave?"

"Seven."

"Forgive the indelicacy," Rudolfi went on, "but how do
you make your hair look like that?"

"I put brilliantine on it. May I ask why all this . . ."

"Heavens, no reason at all," replied Rudolfi. "I was just
curious." Then he added: "Interesting; the man went to a
parish school, he shaves every day and lies on the floor beside
the oil stove. You're an odd customer!" Then he sharply
changed his tone and said sternly: "The censorship will never
pass your novel and no one will print it. *Dawn* won't take it,
nor will *Aurora!*"

"I know that," I said firmly.

"Nevertheless I'm going to take it," said Rudolfi (my heart
turned a somersault), "and I'll pay you (here he named an
incredibly small sum, I forget how much) per page. Tomorrow it will be typewritten."

"There are four hundred pages of it!" I cried hoarsely.

"I'll divide it into parts," said Rudolfi in an iron voice,
"and by tomorrow evening twelve of my typists will have finished transcribing it."

I ceased objecting and decided to obey Rudolfi.

"The typewriting will be at your expense," Rudolfi went
on and I could only nod my head like a dummy. "Now you
must cross out three words on pages one, seventy-one and
three hundred and two."

I looked at the manuscript and saw that the first word
was "apocalypse," the second "archangels" and the third—
"devil." I obediently erased them; I was about to say that

it was childish to cross out these words, but then I looked at Rudolfi and shut up.

"Then," went on Rudolfi, "you'll come with me to the censor's office, where I should be most obliged if you would not utter a single word."

At this I could not help taking offense. "If you think I'm so useless," I began with dignity, "I might as well stay at home."

Rudolfi paid no attention to this attempt to object and continued: "No, you may not stay at home; you will come with me."

"What will I do there?"

"You will sit on a chair," ordered Rudolfi, "and to whatever is said to you, you will respond with a polite smile . . ."

"But . . ."

"And I will do the talking," said Rudolfi in conclusion. He then asked for a clean sheet of paper, wrote a number of lines on it in pencil and made me sign it, then pulled two crackling banknotes out of his pocket, put my manuscript into his pocket and vanished.

I did not sleep all night, walked around the room, looked at the banknotes in the light, drank some cold tea and imagined to myself the bookshop counters. People were crowding into the shops asking for this issue of the magazine. In their homes people were sitting under their lamps reading it.

My God! How stupid it was, how stupid! But I was still young then, you shouldn't laugh at me.

CHAPTER FIVE

UNUSUAL EVENTS

STEALING things is easy. Putting them back again is
much harder. With the Browning and its holster in my
pocket I arrived at my friend's apartment.

My heart gave a jump when I heard him shout through the
door, "Mother! Who is it this time? . . ."

The muffled voice of his old mother replied, "The
plumber."

"What's happened?" I asked as I took off my overcoat.

My friend glanced around him and whispered, "Somebody
has pinched my revolver, damn them!"

"Oh dear, dear," I said.

His old mother was shuffling around their small apartment,
crawling on the passage floor, peering into a basket.

"Don't be silly, mother. Stop crawling about on the floor."

"Did it happen today?" I said cheerfully. (He was wrong, the revolver had disappeared yesterday, but for some reason or other he was sure he had seen it on the table yesterday evening.) "Who has been in here?"

"The plumber!" shouted my friend.

"Parfyon dear, he didn't go into your study," said the old woman timidly, "he went straight to the tap."

"Oh, mother, mother!"

"Wasn't anybody else here? What about yesterday?"

"Nobody came yesterday! Only you, and nobody else." Suddenly my friend turned his stare onto me.

"I beg your pardon," I said with dignity.

"Oh, you intellectuals, you take offense so easily," my friend shouted. "I didn't think you'd stolen it."

Then we went to look and see which tap the plumber had come to mend. While we did so, his mother acted the plumber's part and even imitated his tone of voice.

"He came in like this, you see," said the old woman, "said 'good morning,' hung up his cap and went . . ."

"He went where?"

Imitating the plumber, the old woman went into the kitchen, my friend hurrying after her; I made a movement if to follow them, but instead went straight back into study, put the revolver into the right-hand, not the left-hand drawer of the desk and returned to the kitchen.

Back in the study I asked sympathetically: "Where do you keep it?"

My friend opened the left-hand drawer and pointed to the empty place.

"I don't understand it," I said, shrugging my shoulders. "It really is most odd. Yes, it's obviously been stolen."

My friend went completely crazy.

"And yet, I can't help thinking that it wasn't stolen," I said after a while. "After all, if nobody was here, who could have taken it?"

My friend jumped up from his seat and went through the pockets of an old overcoat hanging in the hall. He found nothing.

"Yes, clearly someone has stolen it," I said thoughtfully. "You'll have to tell the police."

My friend gave a groan.

"I suppose you didn't put it away somewhere else?"

"I always put it in the same place!" shrieked my friend edgily, opening the middle desk drawer as proof. Then he muttered something, opened the left-hand drawer and even thrust his hand into it, into the lower drawer underneath it and then he swore and opened the right-hand drawer.

"My God!" he screamed, looking at me. "Well, how d'you like that? Mother! I've found it."

He was unusually cheerful for the rest of that day and made me stay to supper.

Having dealt with the revolver problem, which had been weighing on my conscience, I took what some might think was a risky step. I gave up my job at the *Shipping Gazette*.

I entered another world. I saw quite a lot of Rudolfi and began to meet writers, some of whom were very well known. But now all that has somehow been blurred in my memory, leaving nothing but a feeling that it was all vaguely disagreeable; I have forgotten it all. One thing only I cannot forget— my meeting with Rudolfi's publisher, Macarius Rvatsky. Rudolfi had everything: intelligence, flair, even a certain erudition, but he lacked just one thing—money. Nevertheless Rudolfi was driven on by a passionate love of his risky job to do anything, at no matter what cost, to publish his famous magazine. I really believe that without it he would have died.

It was for this reason that one day I found myself in a curious building on one of the Moscow boulevards. This, Rudolfi explained, was the office of his publisher, Rvatsky. I was surprised to note that the sign hanging outside the entrance to the building announced that this was a "Photographic Equipment Depot." Stranger still was the fact that apart from a few scraps of cotton cloth wrapped up in newspaper there was no "photographic equipment" there at all. The place was seething with people, all wearing overcoats and hats and talking animatedly. In passing I caught two words—"wire" and "jars"—which astounded me, but the people were just as astounded at the sight of me. I said that I had to see Rvatsky on business. I was at once led with great politeness behind a plywood partition, where my amazement increased beyond bounds.

On Rvatsky's desk was an enormous pile of tins of sprats. I liked Rvatsky himself even less than the sprats in his publishing office. Rvatsky was a thin, short, desiccated little man dressed, to my eyes accustomed to the modest clothes worn at the *Gazette,* in most peculiar fashion. He wore a morning coat and check trousers; he had on a dirty starched collar and a green tie with a ruby stickpin. If Rvatsky astonished me, I clearly terrified Rvatsky, or rather confused him, when I explained that I had come to sign a contract with him for my novel which was going to be printed in the magazines he published. However, he quickly pulled himself together, took the two copies of the contract which I had brought, drew out a fountain pen and signed both copies, hardly glancing at them and handed me back both copies and the fountain pen. I had just picked up the pen when I happened to glance at one of the tins marked "Selected Astrakhan Sprats," with a picture of a fisherman with rolled-up trousers standing beside a net, and I suddenly had an agonizing thought.

"Will you pay me the money right away, as it says in the contract?" I asked.

Rvatsky was transformed into one great smile of sweetness and courtesy. He coughed and said, "In exactly two weeks from now; things are a little tight at the moment . . ."

I put down the pen.

". . . or in a week," Rvatsky said hastily. "Why won't you sign?"

"In that case we'll sign the contract together," I said, "when things are not so tight."

Shaking his head, Rvatsky smiled bitterly.

"Don't you trust me?" he inquired.

"My dear sir!"

"All right, then, on Wednesday," said Rvatsky, "if you need the money."

"I'm sorry, I can't wait till then."

"You must sign the contract," said Rvatsky judiciously, "then I might be able to produce the money on Tuesday."

"I'm sorry, I can't." With that I pushed the contract away and started buttoning up my coat.

"One moment. Oh, what a man you are!" exclaimed Rvatsky. "And they say that writers are supposed to be impractical people!"

Suddenly a look of misery came over his pale face, he looked anxiously around and at that moment a young man came in and gave Rvatsky a cardboard ticket wrapped in white paper. "That ticket is a seat reservation," I thought, "he's going away somewhere."

A blush spread over the publisher's cheeks and his eyes sparkled; I had no idea what this could mean. To cut a long story short, Rvatsky gave me the amount stipulated in the contract and wrote out drafts for the balance. For the first and last time in my life I held in my hand a bank draft made out to me. Somebody had to be sent out to fetch the draft forms while I waited, sitting on some boxes which gave off a most powerful smell of shoe leather. I was very flattered at having these drafts.

The next two months have been effaced from my memory. I only remember that I was annoyed with Rudolfi for sending me to a man like Rvatsky, because I felt that a publisher with such shifty eyes and a ruby tiepin ought not to exist. I also remember how my heart contracted when Rudolfi said: "Just show me those drafts" and how it stopped completely when he said through clenched teeth: "They're in order." I shall also never forget what happened when I went to cash the first of the drafts. To begin with, the sign "Photographic Equipment Depot" had vanished and had been replaced by one saying: "Pharmaceutical Containers Depot."

I entered and said, "I have to see Macarius Borisovich Rvatsky."

I well remember how my legs went weak when I was told that Macarius Borisovich Rvatsky was . . . abroad.

Oh, my heart! Still, none of it matters any longer now. This time Rvatsky's brother was behind the partition. (Rvatsky had gone abroad ten minutes after signing the contract with me—remember the seat reservation?) Aloysius Rvatsky, in appearance the complete opposite of his brother—athletically built, a grave expression—cashed my draft. Two months later, cursing, I had to cash the second draft at some official institution where you claim on unpaid bills of exchange—a notary's office, I think, or a bank: there were bars on the windows. I was more cunning about the third draft; I went to see Rvatsky the Second two weeks before it was due and said that I was tired of waiting. Rvatsky's gloomy brother turned his gaze on me for the first time and mumbled, "I see. But why wait until they're due? You could have the money now."

Instead of eight hundred rubles I got four hundred and with great relief handed Rvatsky the two oblong bills. Ah, Rudolfi, Rudolfi! Thank you for Macarius and Aloysius! However let's not anticipate; it gets even worse later on.

Meanwhile I bought myself an overcoat and finally came a day of severe frost when I went back to that same office. It was evening. A hundred-candle-power bulb hurt my eyes beyond endurance. Neither of the Rvatskys was to be found under the lamp behind the plywood screen (needless to say, Rvatsky the Second had decamped too!). Beneath the lamp stood Rudolfi in his overcoat and in front of him on the desk, on the floor and under the desk lay the blue-gray copies of the newly printed issue of his magazine. Oh, that moment! It all seems ridiculous now, but I was younger then.

Rudolfi's eyes were shining. Like a true editor, he loved his job.

There is a certain sort of young man you must have seen about Moscow. They hang around editorial offices on publication day, but they are not writers; they are at every theater for the dress rehearsals, although they are not actors; they go to art exhibitions, but they do not paint. They refer to operatic prima donnas by their first names, as they do to many other public figures whom they have never so much as met. At premières at the Bolshoi, pushing their way between the seventh and eighth rows they wave to someone in the dress circle; at the Metropole they are to be found sitting at little tables right by the fountain and the multi-colored bulbs light up their wide-bottomed trousers.

One of them was sitting in front of Rudolfi.

"Well, how do you like this issue?" Rudolfi asked the young man.

"Ilya Ivanovitch!" exclaimed the young man in quivering tones, twisting the copy in his hands, "It's a splendid issue, but Ilya Ivanovitch, I must say in all frankness that we, the readers, fail to understand how a man of your taste could have printed that piece by Maxudov."

Chilled, I thought, "Now we're in for a scene," but Rudolfi gave me a conspiratorial wink and said, "What's wrong with it?"

"What's wrong with it!" exclaimed the young man; "Well, firstly . . . may I be frank with you, Ilya Ivanovich?"

"Please do, please do," said Rudolfi, beaming.

"Firstly, it's full of elementary mistakes in grammar. I could underline twenty passages with the most crass errors!"

("I must read it through at once," I thought, feeling faint.)

"And then the style!" shouted the young man. "My God, what appalling style! Anyway, it's eclectic, imitative and flabby. Cheap philosophizing, skating over the surface of things. . . . It's dreary and it's bad. Ilya Ivanovich! Apart from that he's imitating someone else."

"Whom?" asked Rudolfi.

"Averchenko!" screamed the young man, twisting and turning the copy and tearing the uncut pages with his finger. "It's just a piece of Averchenko, at his most uninspired. Look, I'll show you . . ." Here the young man began leafing through the copy, while I, my neck sticking out like a goose, watched his hands. Unfortunately he could not find what he was looking for.

("I'll find it at home," I thought.)

"I'll find it at home," said the young man. "The issue is ruined, you know, Ilya Ivanovich. The man is simply illiterate. Who is he? Where did he go to school?"

"He says he was educated at a parish school," replied Rudolfi, his eyes gleaming. "But why don't you ask him yourself? Allow me to introduce you . . ."

Something like a green putrescent mold spread over the young man's cheeks and his eyes filled with inexpressible horror. I bowed to him, he bared his teeth mirthlessly, pain distorted his pleasant features. He groaned and pulled a handkerchief out of his pocket and then I noticed that blood was running down his cheek. I went rigid.

"What's the matter?" cried Rudolfi.

"A nail," replied the young man.

"Well, I'm off," I said in a strangled voice, trying not to look at the young man.

"Take your copies."

I collected a parcel of authors' free copies, shook Rudolfi by the hand, bowed to the young man—still pressing his handkerchief to his cheek, he had dropped the magazine and his stick to the floor—backed toward the door, hit my elbow against the desk and went out. Thick, Christmassy snow was falling. There is no point in describing how I sat up all night over the magazine, rereading various passages of my novel. It is worth noting that there were times when I liked it, only to find it repulsive a moment later. By morning I was horrified by it.

I well remember the events of the following day. In the morning my friend, whom I had successfully robbed, came to call on me and in the evening I went to a party arranged by a group of writers to celebrate a very important event—the safe return from abroad of the famous author Ismail Alexandrovich Bondarevsky. The brilliance of the occasion was increased by it also being a celebration to mark the return of another well-known writer—Yegor Agapenov—from a visit to China.

I dressed and set off for the party in great excitement. It represented, after all, the new world in which I was striving for acceptance. Not only was that world about to open up before me, but I would see it in its most brilliant aspect—the party was to include the very flower of literary society. I was not mistaken, for as I entered my heart leaped with delight. The first person I saw was that same young man of yesterday who had lacerated his ear with a nail. I recognized him even though he was completely swathed in gauze bandages. He was as overjoyed to see me as if I had been his brother, shook me lengthily by the hand and added that he had been reading my novel all night and that he had come to like it.

"I read it all night, too," I said to him, "but I started to hate it." We chatted away on the warmest terms, the young man telling me that the menu was to include sturgeon in aspic; he was thoroughly cheerful and excited.

I looked around. The new world had admitted me and I liked it. The apartment was enormous. The table was set for about twenty-five; crystal glasses flashed in the light, even the black caviar seemed to be sparkling; fresh green cucumbers aroused rather silly but gay memories of distant picnics and, for some reason, thoughts of fame and glory. At this point I was introduced to a very famous author, Lesosekov, and to a short-story writer called Tunsky. A few women, though not many, were at the party. Likospastov was a very subdued figure and I sensed that he was in a class below the rest, that he was not to be compared with the much younger Lesosekov with his curly red hair, to say nothing of Agapenov or Ismail Alexandrovich. Likospastov pushed his way through to me and we exchanged greetings.

"Well, well, well," said Likospastov, sighing for some reason. "I congratulate you sincerely. And let me tell you— you're a clever one. I would have bet my right arm you would never get your novel printed; it looked impossible. How you managed to get to work on Rudolfi I'll never know. I predict

you'll go far. Yet you're as quiet as a mouse to look at . . .
However, still waters . . ."

Just then Likospastov's congratulations were interrupted
by a loud ring at the front door and Konkin, a critic, who was
acting as host (the party was being held in his apartment)
cried out, "Here he is!" It was Ismail Alexandrovich. A resonant voice was heard from the hall, then sounds of kissing,
and a short man wearing a jacket and a celluloid collar entered the dining room. He was shy and embarrassed and he
was clutching a velvet-banded peaked cap, with a dusty mark
where there had once been a civil service badge, which he had
somehow failed to leave in the hall. "There seems to be some
mistake here," I thought at once, because of the obvious dis-
crepancy between the look of the man who had come in and
the hearty laughter and boisterous sounds which had come
from the hall. There had indeed been a mistake. Clasping
him affectionately around the waist Konkin now led into the
dining room a tall, well-built handsome man with a neat, jutting beard and carefully parted curly hair.

One of the guests, an essayist called Fialkov—Rudolfi
whispered to me that his stock was rising fast—was extremely
well dressed (as was everybody else), but Ismail Alexandrovich's attire was incomparably better than Fialkov's. Ismail
Alexandrovich's shapely if stoutish figure was clad in a brown
suit of superb material, made by a first-class Parisian tailor.
Starched shirt, patent-leather pumps, amethyst cuff links. Ismail Alexandrovich looked clean, white, fresh, bright, gay and
unaffected. His teeth flashed and he cried as his gaze passed
over the festive table, "Ha! You devils!"

There was then a burst of laughter, applause and resounding kisses. With one Ismail Alexandrovich shook hands, with
another he exchanged kisses, with a third he jokingly turned
aside, covering his face with a white palm as though blinded
by the sun, snorting with laughter as he did so. He must have
taken me for somebody else, as he kissed me three times. I
noticed that Ismail Alexandrovich smelled of brandy, eau de
cologne and cigars.

"Baklazhanov!" exclaimed Ismail Alexandrovich, pointing to the man who had come in first. "Let me introduce my friend Baklazhanov." Baklazhanov smiled a martyr's smile and was so embarrassed at being among this large crowd of strangers that he put his peaked cap onto the head of a chocolate-colored statue of a maiden holding an electric light in her hands.

"I dragged him here with me," went on Ismail Alexandrovich, "because I didn't see why he should sit at home doing nothing. He's a splendid fellow and a great scholar. Mark my words, he'll be treading on all our heels in a year at the most. What the devil have you put your cap on her for, Baklazhanov?"

Baklazhanov flushed with shame and was just about to make a jerky movement to shake hands, but nothing came of it as there was a sudden boiling whirlpool of people sitting down and a huge glazed dish of fish pie was already circulating as people milled around finding their places.

The banquet proceeded with an air of gaiety and good cheer. "Tell people they can unbutton!" I heard Ismail Alexandrovich saying. "Why should you and I be the only ones eating with our jackets undone, Baklazhanov?" The clink of crystal caressed our ears and I had the impression that more lights had been turned on in the chandelier. After the third glass all eyes turned toward Ismail Alexandrovich. Somebody begged him, "Tell us about Paris! Tell us about Paris!"

"Well, we went to the automobile show," Ismail Alexandrovich was saying. "The official opening—all very proper: the minister, journalists, speeches . . . that crook Sashka Kondyukov was there among the journalists . . . some Frenchman made a speech . . . short, impromptu speech . . . champagne, of course . . . just as I turned to look, Kondyukov's cheeks bulged out and before anyone could so much as blink he was sick all over the place. In front of ladies —and the minister! And that son-of-a-bitch has to . . . ! What came over him I cannot understand to this day. Colossal scandal! The minister, of course, pretended not to have noticed anything, but how anyone could have failed to notice

. . . Tailcoat, opera hat, trousers costing thousands of francs—ruined! Well, they led him off, gave him a drink of water and drove him home!"

"More! More!" came the cry all around the table.

At this point a maid in a white apron started to serve the sturgeon. The noise grew louder, punctuated by individual voices. In my agonized desire to hear all about Paris I had to strain my ears to catch Ismail Alexandrovich's stories amid all the noise, clatter and exclamations.

"Baklazhanov! Why aren't you eating anything?"

"Go on! Please!" shouted a young man, applauding. "What happened then?"

"Well, after that both these rogues met face to face on the Champs Élysées. Tableau! I hadn't time to look around before that blackguard Katkin spat at him fair and square on the snout!"

"Oh, God!"

"Yes, he did . . . Baklazhanov, wake up, damn you! . . . Well, from sheer agitation—he's fearfully neurotic—he gave a great sweep with his arm and hit some totally unknown woman's hat!"

"On the Champs Élysées?"

"Just imagine. Of course, that sort of thing can easily happen there. And her hat alone cost three thousand francs! Then naturally some bystander hit him in the face with a stick . . . terrible scandal!"

A cork popped in one corner of the room and a narrow glassful of yellow apricot brandy was glittering in front of me. We drank, I remember to Ismail Alexandrovich's health. Then there was more about Paris.

"Quite unperturbed he said, 'How much?' And that *crook*," Ismail Alexandrovich momentarily closed his eyes in horror—"said 'Eight thousand!' So he said, 'There you are!' And he took his hand out of his pocket and thumbed his nose at him!"

"In the Opera?"

"Imagine! In the Opera, of all places! And there were two ministers sitting in the second row."

"Well, what did the other fellow do then?"

"Called him a bastard, of course!"

"Good Lord!"

"Well, they removed them both, it's no problem there . . ."

The party warmed up. Layers of smoke were already billowing over the table. I felt something soft and slippery under my foot and bending down I saw that it was a piece of salmon. How it got there, I had no idea. Laughter drowned Ismail Alexandrovich's words and I never heard the rest of his astounding tales of Paris. I was just starting to muse on the oddness of life abroad when a ring at the door announced the arrival of Yegor Agapenov. Things had by now reached the silly stage. The sound of a piano came from the next room; someone started quietly playing a fox-trot and I saw my young man shuffling around clasping a woman.

With much gaiety and panache in came Yegor Agapenov, followed by a small, yellow, desiccated Chinaman in black-rimmed glasses. Behind the Chinaman was a woman in a yellow dress and a man called Vasily Petrovich.

"Where's our Ismail?" cried Yegor, rushing toward Ismail Alexandrovich, who burst into delighted laughter, shouted, "Ha! Yegor!" and buried his beard into Agapenov's shoulder.

The Chinaman smiled charmingly at everybody, but uttered not a sound, then or later.

"Let me introduce my Chinese friend!" shouted Yegor, having finished kissing Ismail Alexandrovich. From then on the party grew noisy and confused. Some people started dancing awkwardly on the carpet. There was a cupful of coffee on the desk. Vasily Petrovich was drinking brandy. I saw Baklazhanov asleep in an armchair. The air was thick with cigarette smoke. I had a feeling that it was time I started for home.

Completely unexpectedly, I found myself talking to Agapenov. I noticed that as it drew near to three o'clock in the morning he began to show signs of unease. Amid the gloom and smoke he started talking to somebody or other about something and getting, as far as I could make out, nothing but a firm refusal. Slumped in an armchair by the desk I was drinking coffee, unable to understand why I was feeling so peculiar and why Paris suddenly seemed so boring that I no longer even wanted to go there. Then a broad face with thick eyeglasses loomed over me; it was Agapenov.

"Are you Maxudov?" he asked.

"Yes."

"Heard about you," said Agapenov, "Rudolfi told me. I hear they're printing your novel."

"Yes."

"They say it's pretty good. Ah, Maxudov," Agapenov suddenly whispered, with a wink. "Take a look at that creature . . . d'you see him?"

"The one with the beard?"

"That's the one—he's my brother-in-law."

"Is he a writer?" I asked, studying Vasily Petrovich as he drank brandy and smiled a worried, ingratiating smile.

"No. He works for a cooperative at Tetyushi . . . Don't waste time, Maxudov," whispered Agapenov, "you'll regret it. He's an amazing type. He'll be useful to you in your work. You could squeeze ten short stories out of him in one evening, sell them all and make a lot of money. He's an ichthyosaurus! Pure bronze age! Tells the most shattering stories. You'd never believe what he's seen at Tetyushi. Catch him, otherwise somebody else will get him first and spoil him."

Sensing that we were talking about him, Vasily Petrovich put on an even more worried smile and finished his drink.

"The best thing would be . . . I know what!" croaked Agapenov, "I'll introduce you . . . Are you a bachelor?" he asked anxiously.

"Yes, I am," I said, staring at Agapenov. Joy came over Agapenov's face.

"Marvelous! You make friends with him and then you can take him to your place for the night. Brilliant idea! Have you got a couch of some sort? He'll sleep on the couch and he'll be fine. In two days' time he'll go."

I was so taken aback that all I could say was: "I have a couch . . ."

"Is it wide?" asked Agapenov urgently.

By this time I had pulled myself together a bit—only just in time, because Vasily Petrovich was starting to fidget in obvious anxiety to be introduced to me and Agapenov was pulling me by the arm.

"I'm sorry," I said, "unfortunately I simply can't take him with me. I live in a room which is a passage in someone else's apartment and the owner's children sleep behind a screen . . ." I wanted to add that the children had scarlet fever, then I decided that that would be piling it on too much, but I said it all the same, "And they've got scarlet fever."

"Vasily!" shouted Agapenov. "Have you had scarlet fever?"

How many times in my life have I heard the word "intellectual" applied to me! I admit that I had probably deserved that miserable title. But now I summoned up all my strength and Vasily Petrovich only had time to smile imploringly and say "You . . ." before I said firmly to Agapenov, "I categorically refused to take him. I can't."

"Are you sure you can't?" whispered Agapenov, sotto voce, "Somehow? Mm?"

"No, I can't."

Agapenov hung his head, his lips working.

"But he came to see *you*, didn't he? Where's he staying?"

"Yes, he's staying with me, blast him," said Agapenov wearily.

"Well, then . . ."

"My mother-in-law and my sister arrived today; you see, he's a nice chap, but then this Chinaman turned up . . . Blast them all," Agapenov suddenly burst out, "These in-laws. They should have stayed in Tetyushi . . ."

And with that Agapenov left me.

A vague feeling of disquiet overcame me and without saying goodbye to anybody except Konkin I left the apartment.

CHAPTER SIX

CATASTROPHE

T H I S will be, I think, the shortest chapter. At dawn I felt a chill run down my back. It came again. I hunched myself up and slid my head under the blankets, which made me feel better, but only for a moment. I suddenly felt hot, then so cold that my teeth started chattering. I had a thermometer. It showed a hundred. I was ill.

It was quite late before I managed to go to sleep; I shall never forget that morning. I had just closed my eyes when a bespectacled face leaned over me and muttered, "Take him," and I could only repeat, "No, I won't." I was half dreaming about Vasily Petrovich, half imagining that he was really in my room and the horror of it was that he poured himself out some brandy, which I drank. Paris was unbearable; I was in

the Opera and someone was thumbing his nose. Taking out
his hand, thumbing his nose and putting his hand back in his
pocket . . . Taking out his hand, thumbing his nose . . .

"I'm going to tell the truth," I mumbled when it was already broad daylight behind the grubby, unwashed blind,
"the whole truth. I saw a new world yesterday and it was
repulsive. I won't belong to it. It's a strange world. A disgusting world. I must keep this an absolute secret. Sshhh!" My
lips grew dry unusually quickly. For some reason I put a copy
of the magazine beside me, intending to read it, I suppose,
but I read nothing. I meant to take my temperature again,
but I did not. The thermometer was lying beside me on the
chair, but somehow I had to get up and go somewhere to find
it. After that oblivion set in. I remember the fact of one of
my colleagues from the *Gazette* and the vague features of the
doctor. I had, in fact, a severe bout of influenza. For several
days I wallowed in a fever and then my temperature dropped.
I stopped seeing the Champs Élysées, nobody was spitting at
anybody's hat any more and Paris ceased to stretch out for
hundreds of miles.

I felt hungry again and my kind neighbor cooked me some
broth. I drank it out of a cup with a broken handle, tried to
read my own work but gave up after ten lines or so. On about
the twelfth day I was fit again. I was surprised at having
heard nothing from Rudolfi, although I had written him a
note asking him to come and see me. On the twelfth day I
left the house, went to the "Pharmaceutical Containers Depot" and saw that the door was fastened with a large padlock.
Then I took a long streetcar ride, holding fast to the rail from
weakness and breathing on the frost-covered window. I arrived at Rudolfi's house and rang the bell. No one opened. I
rang again. A little old man opened the door and glared at me
with disgust.

"Is Rudolfi in?"

The old man looked at the toes of his bedroom slippers
and replied: "No, he's not."

When I asked where he had gone, when he would be back

and even, stupidly, why the Depot was padlocked, the old man hesitated, then inquired who I was. I explained everything, including my novel. The old man then said, "He left for America a week ago."

God knows where Rudolfi had really gone and why. What had become of the magazine, the Depot, what was all this about America, how had he gone? I have no idea and never shall. Who, for that matter, was this nasty old man? Weakened by flu, the thought even flashed across my exhausted brain that I had dreamed the whole thing—Rudolfi himself, my novel being published, the Champs Élysées, Vasily Petrovich and the ear scratched by a nail. But on returning home there were the nine copies of the magazine. The novel had been published. It really had. There it was.

Unfortunately I knew none of the other contributors to that issue, so I could not inquire after Rudolfi through them. I made another journey to the Depot, where I was able to convince myself that it no longer even existed; in its place was a café with little oilcloth-covered tables.

Would somebody mind telling me what had happened to several hundred copies of that magazine? Where were they? Never in all my life has there been anything quite so mysterious as the incident of Rudolfi and my novel.

IN SUCH odd circumstances the most sensible thing seemed to be to forget it all, to stop thinking about Rudolfi and about the copies of the magazine which had vanished with him. I did so, but this did not absolve me from the cruel necessity of earning a living. I examined my past.

"Well," I said to myself as I sat over the oil stove during a March snowstorm, "I have lived in the following worlds: world number one—the university laboratory, from which I remember the fume chamber and retorts on stands. I left that world during the Civil War. Let's not argue whether I acted thoughtlessly or not. After a series of unlikely adventures (and yet why call them unlikely—after all, who didn't go through the most improbable adventures during the Civil War?) I then got a job on the *Shipping Gazette*. Why? Let's be frank. I nursed ambitions of becoming a writer. What then? I left the world of the *Gazette*. A new world opened up and when I plunged into it that ghastly party proved it to be unbearable. Whenever I think of Paris a sort of convulsion goes through me and I am momentarily paralyzed. And then that awful Vasily Petrovich! Why didn't he stay in Tetyushi? And gifted though Ismail Alexandrovich may be, he behaved disgustingly in Paris. Had I apparently finished up in a kind of vacuum? I had."

All right then, sit down and write another novel, since you've made it your job and this time you can do it without going to parties. The parties, however, were an excuse; the fact was that I had not the least idea what to write about in my second novel. What was to be my message to humanity? That was the real problem. As for my first novel, no one, let's face it, had read it. They couldn't read it because Rudolfi had disappeared, having clearly failed to get the issue distributed. Even my friend, to whom I had given a copy, had not read it either, I'm sure. Incidentally, I feel certain that having read this, many people are going to call me a "neurotic intellectual." Intellectual I may be, but as for that first word I warn you quite seriously that you are wrong. There is not a trace of neurosis in me. And before you throw that word around you should find out more precisely what it means, by listening to Ismail Alexandrovich's stories. But that's by the way.

First of all I had to live and that meant earning some money, so I stopped daydreaming and looked for a job. At this point life took me by the scruff of the neck and returned me to the *Shipping Gazette* like a prodigal son. I told the manager that I had been writing a novel. He was not impressed. Briefly, we agreed that I was to write four articles a month in return for the union minimum wage. This provided some sort of a material basis for living. My plan was to get these articles off my chest as quickly as possible and start free-lance writing again at night.

I managed the first part of the arrangement all right, but God knows what went wrong with the second. First I went around the bookshops and bought the works of my contemporaries. I wanted to know what they were writing about, how they wrote and what was the magic secret of their trade. I spent recklessly, buying only the very best that was on the market. Heading the list were the works of Ismail Alexandrovich, a book by Agapenov, two novels by Lesosekov, two collections of short stories by Florian Fialkov and much more besides. As my first duty I naturally plunged into Ismail Alexandrovich. A nasty foreboding seized me at my first sight of the dustcover. The book was called *Parisian Trifles*. From the first trifle to the last they turned out to be all too familiar. I read all about the beastly Kondyukov who had vomited at the automobile show, about the other two who had quarreled on the Champs Élysées (one, it appeared, was called Pomadkin and the other Sherstyanikov) and about the scandalmonger who thumbed his nose in the Opera. To give him his due Ismail Alexandrovich wrote with unusual brilliance and planted in me a feeling of something like horror for Paris.

Agapenov had apparently managed to publish a book of short stories in the time that had elapsed since the party— *Tetyushi Homosis*. It was an easy guess that Vasily Petrovich had failed to find anywhere else to spend the night, had slept at Agapenov's and that it had been Agapenov who had exploited the story of his homeless brother-in-law. It was all quite obvious, except for the totally incomprehensible word "homosis."

I twice started reading Lesosekov's novel *The Swans*, twice read as far as page forty-five and had to start again at the beginning because I had forgotten how the book began. This really worried me. Putting Lesosekov aside I started on Fialkov, then on Likospastov. Here I stumbled on a real surprise; as I was reading a story that described a certain journalist (the story was called *The Model Lodger*) I recognized a torn sofa with a protruding spring, a wet patch on the table . . . in other words the story was describing—me. The same trousers, head hunched between shoulders and wolflike eyes —in a word, it was me! Yet I swear by all that I hold dear that the description was unfair. I am not cunning, not greedy, not sly, not a liar and not a careerist and I never said any of the rubbish that was in that story! My chagrin was indescribable as I read Likospastov's story and I determined to keep a much sharper eye on myself. For that decision at least I am very much obliged to Likospastov.

However, these sorrowful musings on my imperfection were nothing compared to the awful realization that I had gained precisely nothing from reading the books of the very best writers; no avenues had opened up, no light gleamed ahead and it had done nothing but depress me. Wormlike, the awful thought began to gnaw at my heart that I should never make a writer. And then came an even more terrible thought: how . . . well, just how does someone like Likospastov get published? I'll be bold and go further—how does someone like Agapenov get into print? Homosis? What on earth is homosis? Pure rubbish!

That March went out like a lion and one day the storm woke me up. As before, I woke up in tears. What a fool I felt! Again there were those same people, again that distant city, the side of a grand piano, the sound of shots and again someone falling in the snow. Born in a dream, these people were now emerging from their dream and coming firmly to life in my cell-like room. There was obviously no getting away from them. But what was I to do with them?

At first I simply talked to them and then I somehow found myself taking the copy of my novel out of the drawer. In the evenings I began to feel that something colored was emerging from the white pages. After staring at it and screwing up my eyes I was convinced that it was a picture—and a picture that was not flat but three-dimensional like a box. Through the lines on the paper I could see a light burning and inside the box those same characters in the novel were moving about. It was a delightful game and more than once I regretted that my cat was dead and there was no one to whom I could show these people moving about in that tiny little room. I was sure the creature would have stretched out his paw and patted the page. I imagined the curiosity burning in his feline eyes, his claw scratching at the lines of print.

After a while noises began coming from the room inside

the book. I could distinctly hear the sounds of a piano. Of course, if I had told this to anybody I suppose they would have advised me to see a doctor. They would have said that someone was playing the piano downstairs and they might even have told me exactly what they were playing. I would have paid no attention. No; someone was playing on my table: I could distinctly hear the gentle sound of piano chords. But that was not all. Whenever the house grew quiet and nobody could have been playing anything I used to catch the heartrending strains of an accordion through the storm, mingling with plaintive unhappy voices. They were certainly not coming from downstairs. Why did the little room grow dark, why did the pages fill with a winter's night by the Dnieper, why those horses' heads and above them men's faces under sheepskin hats? I could see their sharp swords, hear them as they whistled through the air.

There—there was a man, panting as he ran. Through the tobacco smoke I followed him as he went and by straining my eyes I could see that he was being chased . . . There was a shot . . . with a groan he fell headlong as though knifed in the heart. He lay motionless and something black was trickling from his head. High above was the moon and a red line of telltale fires burned in the distant village.

I could have watched the page play this game forever . . . But how was I to pin down those little figures so that they would never run away from me?

One night I decided to describe that enchanted little room. How was I to do it?

It was very simple. What I saw, I wrote down; what I didn't see, I left out. There was the scene: the lights came on and lit it up in bright colors. Did it please me? Extremely. So I'll write that down—Scene One. It's evening, the lamp is burning; it has a fringed shade. Music lies open on the grand piano. Someone is playing *Faust*. Suddenly *Faust* stops and a guitar starts playing. Who is playing it? Here he comes, with the guitar in his hands. I hear him start singing. So I write: "Starts to sing."

I was fascinated by this game. No need now to go to parties, no need to go to the theater. I spent three nights playing around with the first scene and by the end of the third night I realized that I was writing a play.

By April, when the snow had melted out-of-doors, I had knocked the first scene into shape. My heroes were moving about, walking and talking.

At the end of April came Ilchin's letter.

Now that the reader knows how I came to write my novel, I can continue the story from the moment when I met Ilchin.

CHAPTER EIGHT

THE GOLDEN HORSE

"Yes," said Ilchin, screwing up his eyes cunningly and enigmatically, "I have read your novel."

I stared at my companion, who seemed at one moment to be lit by a flickering light, at the next, in shadow. Water lashed at the windowpanes. For the first time in my life I was face to face with one of my readers.

"But how did you get hold of it? I mean, the book . . ." I pointed to my novel.

"Do you know Grisha Aivazovsky?"

"No."

Ilchin raised his eyebrows in amazement.

"Grisha runs the literary department of the Cohort of Friends."

"What on earth is that?"

Ilchin was so amazed that he waited for the next flash of lighting to look me up and down.

"The Cohort is a theater. Haven't you ever been there?"

"I've never been to any theaters. I haven't been in Moscow for very long, you see."

The storm had slackened and daylight was beginning to return. I could see that I was arousing in Ilchin a feeling of amused astonishment.

"Grisha was delighted," said Ilchin in a voice of even greater mystery, "and gave me his copy. It's a magnificent novel."

Not knowing how to behave on such occasions I gave Ilchin a bow.

"And do you know what occurred to me?" whispered Ilchin, closing his left eye in mysterious complicity. "You must turn that novel into a play."

"The finger of fate!" I thought to myself and said, "As it happens, I've already begun to write the play."

Ilchin was so astounded that he started scratching his left ear with his right hand and frowned even harder. At first he seemed unable to believe such a coincidence, but he mastered himself.

"Splendid, splendid! You must go on with it, don't stop for a second. Do you know Misha Panin?"

"No."

"He's our literary editor."

"Aha . . ."

Ilchin went on to say that since only a third of the novel had so far been printed and he desperately wanted to know how it finished, I should have to read the rest of it in manuscript to himself and Misha, as well as to Eulampia Petrovna. Having learned from experience he refrained from asking me whether I knew her but added without prompting that the lady was a theatrical producer.

I was thrilled by Ilchin's plans. He whispered, "You write your play and we'll put it on. Won't that be marvelous, eh?"

My heart leaped, I felt drunk with excitement and anticipation. Ilchin said, "And who knows, stranger things have happened—perhaps the old man himself may decide to produce it! Think of that!"

When he realized that I didn't know the old man either he nodded, while his eyes said, "What a child of nature!"

"Ivan Vasilievich!" he whispered. "Ivan Vasilievich! Do you mean to tell me you don't know him? Haven't you heard that he runs the Independent?" And he added, "Well, well, well!"

My head was already spinning; the world was turning into an exciting place. As if in a distant vision I pictured this new world and I was part of it.

Ilchin and I went out of his office and crossed the room with the fireplace; it seemed transformed. The sky cleared and a sudden ray of light fell on to the parquet. We then passed a mysterious, heavily draped doorway and seeing how much it intrigued me Ilchin seductively beckoned me inside. The sound of our footsteps ceased; we were in silence and subterranean gloom. I was rescued by the guiding hand of my companion and an extended oblong of artificial light filled the chamber—Ilchin had opened some more double doors—and we found ourselves in a small auditorium with about three hundred seats. Two chandeliers glowed dimly beneath the ceiling, the curtain was opened and the stage gaped. It was solemn, enigmatic and empty. Its corners were filled with darkness, but in the middle, faintly gleaming, there stood a golden horse rearing up on its hind legs.

"We are closed today," Ilchin whispered solemnly, as if in church; then he appeared by my other ear and went on, "Our young actors will work on your little play here—what could be better? This theater may look small to you, but in fact it's big and it's always sold out. And if we manage to humor the old man, who knows but he may transfer it to the big stage!"

"He's flattering me," I thought as my heart jumped and trembled with foreboding. But why was he talking such nonsense? Who cared whether the box-office takings were good or not? What mattered was this golden horse and even more important was this fascinating and mysterious "old man" who had to be humored if a play was to be put on . . .

"This is my world!" I whispered, not noticing that I had begun to talk aloud.

"What?"

"Oh, nothing."

When I left Ilchin I was carrying a note from him which read:

DEAR PYOTR PETROVICH,

Please be sure to arrange a ticket for *The Favorite* for the author of *Black Snow*.

Yours,
ILCHIN.

"That is known as a pass," Ilchin explained to me and I left the building carrying the first free pass of my life.

From that day onward my life changed abruptly. By day I worked feverishly on my play. The scenes no longer seemed to be the size of the pages: they expanded to the dimensions of the Academy Stage.

In the evening I waited impatiently to see the golden horse again.

I cannot say whether *The Favorite* was a good play or a bad one. It did not really interest me. But there was an odd attraction about the production. As soon as the lights went out in the tiny auditorium, music began to play somewhere backstage and the characters entered dressed in eighteenth-century costume. The golden horse stood sideways across the stage, the characters would sometimes enter and sit down around its hooves or conduct passionate dialogues at its head. I reveled in it.

A bitter feeling seized me when the play was over and it was time to go out into the street. I had so much wanted to put on the same sort of costume as the actors and take part in the play. "How marvelous," I thought, "if I were suddenly to walk on stage, with an enormous crooked drunkard's nose, a brown cloak, a cane and snuffbox, and say something very funny." I invented my funny lines, sitting there in that narrow row of seats among the audience. But other people were saying funny things written by somebody else and occasionally the audience would laugh. Nothing that I had ever done before or since would have given me such pleasure as to have appeared on that stage.

To the amazement of the glum and laconic Pyotr Petrovich, sitting behind his guichet labeled "Manager—Academy Stage," I went to *The Favorite* three times; the first time I sat in the second row, the second time in the sixth and the third time in the eleventh. Ilchin kept me regularly supplied with passes and I saw another play in which they wore Spanish costume and where one actor played the servant so comically and with such bravura that I broke out in a gentle sweat of sheer pleasure.

May came and at last Eulampia Petrovna, Misha, Ilchin and I had our meeting. We gathered in a cramped little room in the same building as the Academy Stage. The window was open and the hooting of cars reminded us of the city outside. Eulampia Petrovna turned out to be a masterful woman with a regal expression and diamond earrings, while Misha had an astonishing laugh. He would suddenly start laughing—"Ah, ah, ah,"—at which everybody stopped talking and waited. When he finished laughing he fell silent and seemed to grow suddenly older.

"What sad eyes he has," I began to imagine in my usual morbid way. "He once killed a friend in a duel in Pyatigorsk," I thought, "and now that friend haunts him at night, nodding his head outside the window by moonlight." I liked Misha very much.

All three of them showed unusual patience and at one session I read them the next third of the novel. Suddenly, feeling my conscience pricking me, I stopped and said that the rest of it must be obvious to them. It was late.

My hearers then began talking and although they were speaking Russian, what they said was so peculiar that I was quite unable to understand it.

It was Misha's habit, when discussing something, to walk up and down the room, occasionally stopping abruptly.

"Osip Ivanovich?" asked Ilchin softly, frowning.

"No, no, no," replied Misha, suddenly bursting into laughter. When the laughing fit was over he remembered his murdered friend and aged visibly.

"Any of the old stagers . . . ?" Ilchin began.

"I don't think so," growled Misha.

They went on, "But it wouldn't do for the Galins, nor for the subsidiaries . . ." (that was Eulampia Petrovna).

"Excuse me," Misha began sharply, emphasizing his words with a chopping motion of his hand, "I have been insisting for ages that it's time we put this question to the theater!"

"And what about You-know-who?" (Eulampia Petrovna).

"Yes, and nobody knows how India will react to this sort of thing either," added Ilchin.

"We should put it to them all at a meeting," Ilchin whispered softly, "that's how they do it with the music."

"You know-who!" said Eulampia Petrovna significantly.

At this point my expression must have registered utter despair, because the others broke off their incomprehensible discussion and turned toward me.

"We must beg you, Sergei Leontievich," said Misha, "to have the play ready not later than August . . . It is essential that we can read it in full by the beginning of the season."

I forget what happened for the rest of May. June too is a complete blur in my memory, but I do remember July. It was quite unusually hot. I sat naked, wrapped in a towel, and wrote my play. The more it progressed the more difficult it became. My little box had long ceased to give off any sounds, the novel had somehow gone silent and dead and no one would come to my help. Instead the boxlike shape of the Academy Stage rose before my eyes. My heroes grew, expanded and walked on to that stage boldly enough, but they obviously liked it so much there with the golden horse that they seemed to have no wish to leave the stage and the action went on developing without my being able to put an end to it. Then the hot weather cooled, the glass jug from which I had been drinking boiled water grew empty and I noticed a fly swimming at the bottom of it. It rained, August came. I received a letter from Misha. He was asking about the play.

I seized all my courage and cut the plot short. The play consisted of thirteen scenes.

CHAPTER NINE

BEGINNINGS

Lifting my head I could see above me a frosted-glass globe full of light, in a glass case to one side a silver wreath of colossal dimensions adorned with ribbons and inscribed: "To our beloved Independent Theater from the members of the Moscow Bar . . ." (the final word was illegible); in front of me were rows of smiling actors' faces, no two the same.

In the distance I was aware of silence and occasionally something like a cheerful drone which would be interrupted by a noise like a crowd of people in a bathhouse. As I read my play the show was going on.

As I sat there, constantly wiping my forehead with my handkerchief I noticed a stout, thickset man standing in front of me, clean-shaven with a luxuriant growth of hair on his head. He was standing in the doorway with his eyes fixed on me, as though reflecting on something.

He remains as a mere flash in my memory; everything else around me shifted, glittered and changed. Apart from him my only unchanging recollection was that wreath—I remember that most sharply of all.

So began the reading of my play—not at the Academy Stage but at the Principal Stage of the Independent Theater.

Leaving the theater that evening I had looked around to get my bearings. There, in the center of the city, where the delicatessen store flanks the theater and the shop opposite announces "Trusses and Corsets" stood a wholly inconspicuous building, humpbacked like a tortoise, with cubic, frosted-glass lamps outside it.

Next day I made my first acquaintance with the interior of that building in the autumn twilight. I remember walking along a soft broadcloth carpet around something which was, I think, an auditorium and crowds of people passed me as in a dream. The season was beginning.

On I went along the soundless carpet and arrived at an office, charmingly furnished, where I found an equally charming elderly gentleman with clean-shaven chin and a cheerful expression. This was the man in charge of the selection of new plays—Anton Antonovich Knyazhevich.

Over Knyazhevich's desk hung a bright, cheerful picture; it showed a curtain with crimson tassels and beyond the curtain a gay, pale-green garden . . .

"Ah, comrade Maxudov!" cried Knyazhevich in welcoming tones, putting his head on one side, "We've been waiting for you, waiting for you! Please sit down, sit down!"

I sat down in a very comfortable leather armchair.

"I've heard, I've heard your play," said Knyazhevich smiling and spreading his hands as he did so. "A bee-utiful play. Of course we've never put on a play like this one before, but we'll take this one, yes, and we'll put it on, we'll put it on . . ."

The more Knyazhevich spoke the jollier became his expression.

"... and you'll grow terribly rich!" Knyazhevich went on. "You'll ride in a carriage! Yes, sir, in a carriage!"

"Still," I thought, "in spite of all this jollity he's a complicated man, this Knyazhevich, very complicated."

And as Knyazhevich waxed more cheerful I, to my own astonishment, grew progressively more tense and uneasy.

After some more chatter, Knyazhevich rang a bell. "I'm just going to send you to Gavriil Stepanovich, right into his very hands, so to speak. A most remarkable man is our Gavriil Stepanovich ... Wouldn't hurt a fly!" However, the uniformed man with green lapels who had entered in answer to the bell said, "Gavriil Stepanovich has not come to the theater yet."

"Ah well, if he hasn't arrived yet, he will," replied Knyazhevich as cheerfully as before, "he'll be here in half an hour at the most, you'll see. Meanwhile you won't be wasting your time if you walk around the theater, look around, amuse yourself, have a cup of tea and a sandwich at the buffet—don't be stingy with the sandwiches or you'll offend our caterer Yermolai Ivanovich."

I went on tour of the theater. Just to walk on the carpet gave me physical pleasure and I was thrilled by the silence and half-darkness that reigned everywhere. It was in this semigloom that I made yet another acquaintance. A man of about my age, thin and tall, came up to me and introduced himself, "Pyotr Bombardov."

Bombardov was an actor of the Indepentent Theater who said that he had heard my play and that in his opinion it was a good play.

Somehow I became friends with Bombardov from that first moment. He struck me as a highly intelligent, observant man.

"Wouldn't you like to see our portrait gallery in the foyer?" asked Bombardov politely.

I thanked him for the offer and we entered the huge foyer, which was also carpeted in gray broadcloth. Several rows of paneling in the foyer were filled with portraits and enlarged photographs in gilded frames.

From the first frame there gazed at us an oil painting of a woman of about thirty with ecstatic eyes, a fluffy fringe and a deep décolleté.

"Sarah Bernhardt," explained Bombardov.

Next to the famous actress was a frame containing the photographic representation of a man with moustaches.

"Andrei Pakhomovich Sevastianov, the Theater's chief lighting technician," said Bombardov politely.

I recognized Sevastianov's neighbor without prompting—it was Molière.

Beyond Molière was a lady wearing a tiny saucerlike beret on the side of her head, a kerchief knotted at her bosom and holding a lace handkerchief in one hand with a protruding little finger.

"Ludmilla Silvestrovna Pryakhina, an actress of our theater," said Bombardov, with a slight sparkle in his eyes. However, with a sideways glance at me, he said no more.

"Excuse me, but who is that?" I asked in astonishment, staring at the cruel features of a man whose curly head was crowned with laurels. The man was in a toga and held a five-stringed lyre.

"The Emperor Nero," said Bombardov and again the sparkle flashed in his eyes and died.

"But why . . . ?"

"By order of Ivan Vasilievich," said Bombardov, keeping a straight face. "Nero was a singer and an artiste."

"I see . . ."

After Nero came Griboyedov, after Griboyedov Shakespeare in a wide starched ruff and after him an unknown man who turned out to be Plisov, who had been in charge of the theater's revolving stage for forty years.

Then followed Mochalov, Zhivokini, Goldoni, Beaumarchais, Stasov, Shchepkin, Maeterlinck. Suddenly there stared at me from a frame a lancer's shako cocked at a jaunty angle, beneath it an aristocratic face, waxed moustaches, the epaulettes of a cavalry major-general, scarlet lapels and a cartouche belt.

"The late Major-General Claudius Alexandrovich Komarovsky-Echappard de Bioncourt, officer commanding His Majesty's Household Regiment of Lancers."

Seeing my interest Bombardov told me about the man: "His story is quite extraordinary. He once came from Petersburg to Moscow for a couple of days, dined at Testov's and happened to come to our theater that evening. Well, he naturally had a seat in the front row, and watched . . . I don't remember what play was running that evening, but eyewitnesses report that during a scene showing a forest something happened to the general . . . the forest at sunset, birdsong at eventide, off stage the sound of village church bells calling to vespers . . . They looked and there was the general dabbing his eyes with his muslin handkerchief. After the show he went up to Aristarkh Platonovich's office. The commissionaire said afterward that as he went into the office, the general said in a fearful strangled voice, 'Teach me what to do!' Well, he and Aristarkh Platonovich were shut in together . . ."

"Excuse me, but who is Aristarkh Platonovich?" I asked.

Bombardov looked at me in amazement, but at once removed the look of astonishment from his face and explained, "Our theater is headed by two directors—Ivan Vasilievich and Aristarkh Platonovich. Are you, if you don't mind my asking, from Moscow?"

"No, I . . . no. Do go on, please!"

". . . closeted together. Nobody knows what they talked about, but we do know that that very night the general sent a telegram to Petersburg which read: 'To His Majesty. Feeling vocation become actor Your Majesty's Independent Theater humbly beg Your Majesty's permission retire from service. Komarovsky-Bioncourt.' "

Amazed, I asked, "And what happened then?"

"There was the most marvelous rumpus," replied Bombardov. "They handed the telegram to Alexander III at two o'clock in the morning. They woke him up especially. There he was in nothing but his nightshirt, his beard, his little cross on a chain round his neck . . . he said: 'Give it here! What's up with my Echappard?' He read and for two minutes he couldn't speak, but simply turned purple and gasped. Then he said: 'Give me a pencil!' And he immediately scribbled a memorandum on the telegram form: 'I never want to see his face in Petersburg again. Alexander.' And went back to sleep. The next day the general turned up promptly at rehearsal time wearing morning coat and trousers. The memorandum was preserved with a coating of varnish and after the revolution the original telegram form was presented to the theater. You can see it in our museum of curios."

"What sort of parts did he play?" I asked.

"Tzars, generals and majordomos in wealthy households," answered Bombardov. "We play a lot of Ostrovsky, you know, and so many of his plays are about the rich merchant class . . . and then we played Tolstoi's *The Power of Darkness* for a long time . . . Well, of course, our manners need a bit of polishing if you know what I mean . . . And he knew all about etiquette—how to offer a lady her handkerchief when she drops it, how to pour wine and so on; and he spoke French perfectly, better than the French . . . And he had another passion: he adored imitating bird noises offstage. When we ran plays that took place in springtime in the country, he would always be sitting in the wings on a stepladder and whistling like a nightingale. Isn't it an extraordinary story?"

"No, I don't agree with you," I exclaimed fervently. "It's so wonderful here in your theater that if I'd been the general I'd have done exactly as he did . . ."

"That's Karatygin, that's Taglioni," Bombardov listed them all as he led me from portrait to portrait. "Catherine the Great, Caruso, Theopanes Prokopovich, Igor Severyanin, Battistini, Euripides, Mrs. Bobylyova our chief seamstress . . ."

At this moment one of the men in green tunics trotted silently into the foyer and announced in a whisper that Gavriil Stepanovich had arrived in the theater. Bombardov broke off in midword, gave me a powerful handshake, then quietly uttered the two enigmatic words, "Be firm." And disappeared somewhere into the semidarkness.

I set off behind the man in uniform who ambled ahead of me, occasionally beckoning me on and smiling a sickly smile. Every ten paces along the walls of the corridor down which we passed were electrically lit notices which read: "Silence! Rehearsal in Progress."

Another uniformed man with a gold pince-nez, who was sitting in a chair at the end of this circular corridor, saw me coming, leaped up and croaked in a whisper, "Good morning, sir!" He flung open a pair of heavy curtains embroidered with the theater's gold cipher "I.T."

I found myself in what seemed to be a luxurious marquee. The ceiling was draped in green silk radiating in folds outward and downward from the middle, where there shone a crystal chandelier. It was furnished in soft, silk-covered furniture. Another pair of curtains and beyond them a door glazed with frosted glass. My new guide with the pince-nez stopped short of the door but made a gesture which meant "Please knock, sir," and at once withdrew.

I knocked gently, grasped the handle which was made in the shape of a silver eagle's head; there was the sigh of a pneumatic spring and the door let me through. I banged my face against yet another pair of draped curtains, panicked, pushed them away from me . . . Where am I, what's happening to me? I pulled myself together, although the whole performance was beginning to scare me out of my wits . . . To my dying day I shall never forget that office in which I was received by Gavriil Stepanovich, the theater's business manager. Hardly had I entered than an enormous clock in the corner to my left struck melodiously and began to play a minuet.

A profusion of lights met my eyes. A green light from the desk—or rather not a desk but a bureau, or rather not a bureau but a highly complex construction with dozens of drawers and pigeonholes for letters; more light from another lamp with a writhing silver stand and an electric cigar lighter.

There was a hellish red glow from beneath a palisander-wood table, on which stood three telephones; a tiny white light from a little table carrying a flat foreign-made type-writer, a fourth telephone and a pile of paper embossed in gold with the monogram "I.T." There was even a light reflected from the ceiling . . .

The office floor was carpeted, but with billiard-cloth instead of broadcloth, on top of which lay an inch-thick cherry-colored rug. A colossal, cushion-covered couch and beside it a Turkish hookah. Outside in central Moscow it was daytime, but not a ray of light, not a sound from the outside world penetrated this office through the window, muffled by three layers of curtains. Here reigned the eternal wisdom of the night; here it smelled of leather, cigars and scent. The warmed air caressed one's face and hands.

On the gold-tooled Morocco leather wall hung a large photographic portrait of a man with an artistic shock of hair, frowning eyes, drooping moustaches and holding a lorgnette in his hands. I guessed that this was either Ivan Vasilievich or Aristarkh Platonovich, but which of the two I did not know.

With a sharp swing of his revolving chair, a shortish man turned around; he wore a black imperial and a moustache pointing up to his eyes like twin arrows.

"My name is Maxudov," I said.

"Excuse me," rejoined my new acquaintance in a high tenor, implying that he would see me in a moment when he had finished reading some papers and . . .

. . . he finished reading his papers, took off a pince-nez suspended from a black cord, wiped his tired eyes and turning his back finally on the bureau, stared at me without a word. He looked me straight and frankly in the eyes, studying me intently in the way people study some newly acquired piece of mechanism. He made no effort to conceal the fact that he was studying me and he even frowned. I averted my eyes—it was no use, I began to fidget on the couch . . . At last I thought "Oh, well" and by making a tremendous effort I returned the man's stare. In doing so I felt a sense of vague resentment toward Knyazhevich.

"How odd," I thought, "either that man Knyazhevich is blind or . . . he said he wouldn't hurt a fly . . . I don't know. Small, deep-set, steely eyes, obviously a man of iron will, diabolical audacity, inflexible determination . . . a French goatee . . . why shouldn't he hurt a fly? He's horribly like the leader of the musketeers in Dumas . . . what was his name? Damn, I've forgotten!"

The continued silence became unbearable, until it was finally broken by Gavriil Stepanovich. He smiled playfully and suddenly squeezed my knee.

"Well, I suppose we'd better sign our little contract, hadn't we?" he said.

A turn on the revolving chair, a turn back—and Gavriil Stepanovich was holding the contract. "Only I don't know—should I sign it without having it agreed by Ivan Vasilievich?" Here Gavriil Stepanovich cast a quick involuntary glance at the portrait.

"Aha! Well, thank God," I thought, "at last I know that that's Ivan Vasilievich."

"Wouldn't it be a mistake?" Gavriil Stepanovich went on. "Well, perhaps in your case!" he gave a friendly smile.

Without a knock the door opened, the curtain was pushed aside and in came a lady with the proud dark face of a southerner and glanced at me. I bowed to her and said, "My name's Maxudov."

The lady gave me a firm, mannish handshake and replied, "Mine is Augusta Menazhraki." She sat down on a stool, took a gold cigarette holder from the pocket of her cardigan, lit a cigarette and began quietly tapping away at the typewriter.

I read the contract, although I frankly admit that I could not understand it and made no attempt to do so. I wanted to say: "Put on my play; I want nothing except to be allowed to come here every day and spend two hours lying on this couch, inhale the honeyed aroma of tobacco, hear the clock strike and dream."

Fortunately I did not say it aloud.

I seem to remember that the contract was liberally dotted with words like "hereinafter" and "whereas" and that every clause began with the words "The Author shall not."

The Author shall not offer his play to any other theater in Moscow.

The Author shall not offer his play to any theater whatsoever in Leningrad.

The Author shall not offer his play to any other town whatsoever in the R.S.F.S.R.

The Author shall not offer his play to any other town whatsoever in the U.S.S.R.

The Author shall not have his play printed.

The Author shall not have the right to make such-and-such a demand of the Theater—what it was, I forget (clause twenty-one).

The Author shall not have the right to protest about something or other (I forget what).

One clause, however, disturbed the monotony of this document—this was clause fifty-seven. It began with the words: "The Author must." In accordance with this clause the author bound himself "unreservedly and without delay to incorporate into the said Work all such corrections, alterations, emendations or abridgments as the Management or any Commission, Institution, Organization, Body Corporate or Natural Person thereunto empowered shall require, for the execution whereof he may demand no emoluments other than those specified in clause fifteen."

In studying this clause I noticed that there was a blank space after the word "emoluments." I questioningly underlined the space with my fingernail.

"What payment would you consider suitable?" asked Gavriil Stepanovich, without taking his eyes off me.

"Knyazhevich told me," I said, "that I would get two thousand rubles . . ."

My vis-à-vis gave a respectful inclination of his head. "I see," he said, paused a while and added: "Ah, money, money! The root of all evil! We all think of nothing but money! But who gives a thought to his soul?"

So far in my hard life I had had no time for such aphorisms and I admit that it caught me slightly off-balance . . . I thought, "Who knows, perhaps Knyazhevich was right about

Gavriil Stepanovich and it's I who am callous and suspicious . . ." As a gesture toward convention, I let out a sigh. My interlocutor replied in turn with a sigh and then suddenly gave me a playful wink, which seemed completely out of keeping with his sigh and he whispered confidentially:

"How about four hundred rubles, eh? Just because it's you—eh?"

I must admit that this annoyed me. The fact was that I hadn't a kopeck to my name and I was counting heavily on that two thousand.

"Eighteen hundred?" I asked. "Knyazhevich said . . ."

"He's trying to curry favor," said Gavriil Stepanovich bitterly.

There was a knock at the door and another man in green uniform brought in a tray covered with a white napkin. The tray was laden with a silver coffeepot, a milk jug, two porcelain cups colored orange outside and gilded inside, two slices of bread and butter with black caviar, two with slices of smoked sturgeon, two with cheese and two with cold roast beef.

"Did you take that parcel to Ivan Vasilievich?" Augusta Menazhraki asked the man who had come in.

The man's expression changed and he tilted the tray.

"I had to go to the buffet, Augusta Avdeyevna, and Ignutov took the parcel," he said.

"I told *you* to do it, not Ignutov," said Madame Menazhraki. "It's not Ignutov's business to take parcels to Ivan Vasilievich. Ignutov's stupid, he'll lose his way or give the wrong message . . . Do you want to send Ivan Vasilievich's temperature up?"

"He wants to kill him," said Gavriil Stepanovich coldly.

The man with the tray groaned softly and dropped a spoon.

"Where was Pakin while you were at the buffet?" inquired Augusta Avdeyevna.

"Pakin went to see about the car," the man explained. "I went to the buffet and said to Ignutov—you run over to Ivan Vasilievich . . ."

"What about Bobkov?"

"Bobkov had gone to see about some tickets."

"Put it down there," said Augusta Avdeyevna; she pressed a button and a table top slid out of the wall.

The uniformed man looked relieved, put down his tray, pushed the curtains aside with his bottom, opened the door with his foot and slipped out.

When he had gone Gavriil Stepanovich turned to me and said confidentially: "How about four hundred and twenty-five rubles?"

Augusta Avdeyevna dug her teeth into her first slice and started quietly typing with one finger.

"Thirteen hundred perhaps? I feel rather embarrassed because I'm out of funds for the moment and I have to pay my tailor . . ."

"The man who made that suit?" asked Gavriil Stepanovich, pointing at my trousers.

"Yes."

"Well, he's a rogue to cheat you off with workmanship like that," said Gavriil Stepanovich. "If I were you I'd tell him off."

"But look here . . ."

"We don't," said Gavriil Stepanovich uncomfortably, "exactly have any precedents for paying our authors in cash on signature of the contract, but in your case . . . four hundred and twenty-five!"

"Twelve hundred," I responded boldly, "I can't manage without it . . . I'm in difficult circumstances . . ."

"Have you tried gambling at the races?" asked Gavriil Stepanovich sympathetically.

"No," I replied, regretfully.

"We had an actor who got into trouble. He went to the races and just imagine—he won fifteen hundred rubles. But I shouldn't follow his example. I can tell you as a friend—it'll burn a hole in your pocket. Ah, money! What's it for? Look —I have none and I couldn't be a happier man . . ." And Gavriil Stepanovich turned out his pocket and showed that he really had no money, nothing but a bunch of keys on a chain.

"A thousand," I said.

"Oh, what the hell!" said Gavriil Stepanovich recklessly. "I don't care what they say to me afterward—I'll give you five hundred rubles. Come on—sign!"

I signed the contract, while Gavriil Stepanovich explained that the money I would be given was an advance on the earnings of the first few performances of the play. We agreed that I would get seventy-five rubles that day, a hundred rubles two days later, another hundred on Saturday and the rest on the fourteenth of the month.

God, how dreary and prosaic the street seemed after that office! It was drizzling, a cart loaded with firewood had got stuck in the gateway to the yard and the carter was yelling blue murder at his horse, people were walking along looking unhappy because of the weather. I floated home, trying not to see the ugly truth of life all around me. I guarded the cherished contract next to my heart.

At my rooms I found my friend (see the story about the revolver).

With wet hands I dragged the contract from where it nestled at my bosom and cried, "Read that!"

My friend read the contract and to my great astonishment lost his temper with me.

"This is nothing but a useless scrap of paper! You must be out of your mind to have signed this!" he shouted.

"You don't know anything about theatrical matters so shut up!" I said, losing my temper too.

"What's all this—'the author must do this, must do that'; *they* apparently aren't obliged to do anything at all," growled my friend.

I started enthusiastically telling him about the picture gallery, how kind Gavriil Stepanovich had been, about Sarah Bernhardt and General Komarovsky. I wanted to tell him how the clock had chimed a minuet, how the coffee had steamed, how magically soft the footsteps had sounded on the carpet, but the clock remained an image in my mind, I could visualize the golden cigarette holder, the hellish glow from the electric fire and even the emperor Nero, but none of it could I describe.

"I suppose it's Nero who writes their contracts?" said my friend with heavy sarcasm.

"Oh, go to hell!" I shouted and tore up the contract in front of him.

We decided to have lunch together and sent Dusya's brother off to the delicatessen. An autumn shower was falling. What ham that was, what butter! Moments of bliss!

The Moscow climate is famous for its changeability. Two days later the weather was beautiful, as warm as a summer's day and I hurried off to the Independent Theater. With a delicious feeling of anticipatory pleasure at the hundred rubles I was due to get, I caught sight of a modest poster as I approached the theater. I read:

Repertoire for the Coming Season

AGAMEMNON	Aeschylus
PHILOCTETES	Sophocles
FENISA'S BAIT	Lope de Vega
KING LEAR	Shakespeare
THE MAID OF ORLEANS	Schiller
NOT OF THIS WORLD	Ostrovsky
BLACK SNOW	Maxudov

I stood openmouthed on the pavement—it was amazing that my pocket wasn't picked. People bumped into me, swore at me and I just went on standing there contemplating the poster. I then moved aside to watch what effect it had on the passing citizenry.

It turned out to have none at all. Unless you count three or four people who glanced at it in passing, nobody actually read it at all.

However, before five minutes had passed I was repaid a hundredfold for my patience. In the stream of people passing the theater I clearly distinguished the powerful head of Yegor Agapenov. He was walking toward the theater with his whole retinue, including Likospastov with a pipe between his teeth

and an unknown man with a fat, pleasant face. Bringing up
the rear was a Negro in an unusual yellow summer overcoat
and for some reason hatless. I shrank further into my niche
where I stood motionless as a statue and watched.

The group drew level with the poster and stopped. I cannot describe what happened to Likospastov. He was the first
to pull up and read the lettering. A smile was playing about
his face, his lips were still moving as he finished telling some
funny story. "He's got as far as *Fenisa's Bait* . . ." Suddenly
Likospastov turned pale and somehow looked older. His expression showed unfeigned horror.

Agapenov read it and said: "Hm . . ."

The fat stranger blinked . . . "He's trying to remember
where he's heard my name . . ."

The Negro started asking his friends in English what they
had seen. Agapenov said: "Poster, poster . . ." and sketched
an oblong shape in the air. The Negro nodded, still none the
wiser.

A horde of people passed them by, now pushing the group
apart, now forcing them closer together. At moments I could
hear what they were saying, then it would be drowned by
street noises.

Likospastov turned to Agapenov and said, "No, really have
you seen this Yegor Nilych? What can it mean?" He looked
around with a miserable expression. "They must have gone
mad! . . ." The wind blew away the end of his sentence.

I could hear snatches of Agapenov's bass alternating with
Likospastov's tenor.

"Who does he think he is? . . . I discovered him, after
all . . . yes, him . . . ugh, a horrible type . . ."

I emerged from my niche and walked straight toward
them.

Likospastov saw me first and I was astounded at the change
which came over his face. Those were Likospastov's eyes, but
there was something new about them, a look of alienation, as
if some gulf lay between us . . .

"Well, my friend," cried Likospastov. "Well, I must say! I
wasn't expecting this. Aeschylus, Sophocles—and you! I don't

know how you managed it, but you've done brilliantly! Of course you won't recognize your old friends any more. We're not quite in the Shakespeare class."

"Do stop talking such rot," I said shyly.

"Words fail me! Well I'm damned! Of course, I'm not a bit jealous. Let me congratulate you, dear boy." I felt the touch of Likospastov's cheek, dotted with wiry stubble.

"Meet my friends."

I was introduced to the fat man, who had not taken his eyes from me. He said, "How d'you do. Name's Krupp."

I was also introduced to the Negro, who said something interminable in broken English. As I couldn't understand a word of it, I said nothing in reply.

"Of course they're going to play it on the Academy Stage, I suppose?" said Likospastov, fishing for information.

"I don't know," I said. "They're talking of putting it on the Principal Stage . . ."

Likospastov turned pale again and looked miserably up at the clear sky.

"Ah, well," he said hoarsely, "I suppose you deserve a bit of luck. Perhaps this will be your first success. The novel was a flop, but who knows, it may click as a play. Don't get too stuck up, though. Remember, there's nothing worse than forgetting your friends."

Krupp was staring at me with an increasingly thoughtful look and I noticed that he was paying the greatest attention of all to my hair and nose.

The moment came to go. It was most embarrassing. As he shook my hand Yegor asked me whether I had read his book. I turned cold with fear and said that I hadn't read it. It was now Yegor's turn to go pale.

"How could he have read it?" said Likospastov. "He hasn't got time to read contemporary literature . . . I'm joking, of course . . ."

"You should read it," said Yegor weightily, "it's turned out to be rather a nice little book."

I went into the theater by the dress circle entrance. A window on to the street was open. A man in a yellow tunic was cleaning it with a rag. I could vaguely see the heads of my literary friends through the frosted glass and heard the sound of Likospastov's voice, "It makes you feel like a fish beating your head against the ice . . . It's sickening!"

The poster was still revolving in front of my mind's eye and I had only one single thought in my head—that my play was, if the truth were told, extremely bad. Something had to be done about it, but God only knew what. At that moment, in the delightful semidarkness of the corridor, I found myself facing the stocky figure of the same man who had stood in the doorway at the reading of the play. He had fair hair, a determined face and an uneasy look. He was carrying a well-stuffed briefcase.

"Comrade Maxudov?" inquired the fair-haired man.

"Yes, that's me . . ."

"I've been looking for you all over the theater," he said, "allow me to introduce myself: Thomas Strizh, producer. Well, everything seems to be in order. Don't get excited and don't get worried, your play is in good hands. Have you signed the contract?"

"Yes."

"Now you're our man," went on Strizh in a decisive voice, his eyes glittering. "I tell you what you should do: you should sign a contract with us for all your future work! For the rest of your life! We must have it all. We could do that at once, if you like. Excuse me!" Strizh turned and spat into a spittoon. "Well now, I shall be producing your play. We'll knock it out in a couple of months and the dress rehearsal will be on December fifteenth. The Schiller won't hold us up; Schiller's no problem . . ."

"I'm sorry," I said timidly, "but I was told that Eulampia Petrovna was going to produce it . . ."

Strizh's expression altered instantly.

"What do you mean, Eulampia Petrovna?" he inquired severely. "Nothing of the sort!" His voice grew metallic. "Eulampia has nothing to do with it. She and Ilchin are going to produce In the West Wing. I have a definite agreement with Ivan Vasilievich. And if anybody tries to do anything behind my back I shall write to India! By registered letter if need be!" Strizh started shouting in a threatening voice, inexplicably overcome with anxiety. "Give me a copy!" he ordered me, thrusting out his hand.

I explained that the play had not yet been transcribed.

"What can they have been thinking of?" exclaimed Strizh, staring around in agitation. "Have you been to see Polixena Toropetzkaya in the changing room?" *

I had no idea what he was talking about and could only stare wildly at Strizh.

"You haven't? Well, it's her day off today. Go and see her tomorrow and get it copied out. Use my name. Don't be put off!"

At this point an elegant man with a guttural, very educated voice appeared and said politely but insistently, "Please come to the rehearsal room, Thomas. We're starting."

Strizh gripped his briefcase under his arm and went off, shouting back to me in farewell, "Go to the changing room tomorrow! Use my name!"

I was left alone and stood for a long time, motionless.

* The Russian word used for "changing room" is "*predbannik*," which specifically means the changing room of a public bathhouse. The room in question has been given this nickname because it is the anteroom to the director's office, and is where the actors must wait before being called in to see the manager—often to be given a reprimand. The pun lies in the fact that the Russian expression "to give someone a bath" is the equivalent of the English "to put someone on the carpet" or give them a severe dressing down. Hence the manager's office is by implication "the bathhouse" and the anteroom "the changing room."

CHAPTER TEN

IN THE
CHANGING ROOM

THE AUTUMN drew on. My play had thirteen scenes. Sitting alone in my room I held my old-fashioned silver watch in front of me and read the play aloud to myself, to the obvious consternation of my next-door neighbor. I noted the time it took to read each scene. When I had finished I worked out that the play had taken three hours to read. I then remembered that plays have to have intervals for the audience to go out to the bar. Adding on the interval times, I realized that my play as it stood was too long to perform in a single evening. The nights of agony caused by this problem forced me to cut out one scene. This shortened the play by twenty minutes, but the situation was far from saved. I remembered, too, that apart from the intervals there were also pauses in the action, such as when, for instance, the actress is standing, crying and arranging some flowers in a vase. She has nothing to say, yet time is flying all the same. Obviously, muttering the dialogue to oneself at home is one thing and speaking it on stage is quite another.

Something else had to be thrown out of the play—but what? It all seemed to me equally vital and I felt, too, as soon as I condemned some part of it to extinction, that the whole laboriously constructed edifice was starting to totter. I dreamed of ceilings collapsing and balconies disintegrating and those dreams seemed agonizingly real.

Then I removed one of the characters. As a result one scene became lopsided and finally it had to go. There were now eleven scenes. After that however much I racked my brains, however many cigarettes I smoked, I simply could not shorten it any further. Every day my left temple ached. Realizing that I was getting nowhere I decided to let things take their natural course and went to see Polixena Toropetzkaya.

"No, I shall never manage it without Bombardov . . ." I thought.

Bombardov, in fact, proved extremely helpful. He explained what people meant when they talked about "India" and what went on in the changing room. At last he made it clear to me that the Independent Theater was run by two directors: Ivan Vasilievich (as I already knew) and Aristarkh Platonovich.

"By the way, tell me something—why is there only *one* portrait, Ivan Vasilievich's, in that office where I signed my contract?"

At this Bombardov, who was usually so self-confident, muttered in embarrassment, "Why? Downstairs? Well . . . er . . . Aristarkh Platonovich . . . his portrait's . . . er . . . upstairs . . ."

I realized that Bombardov wasn't used to me yet and felt uncomfortable with me. This was obvious from his incoherent reply, so I tactfully refrained from pressing the point . . . "This is an entrancing world, but it is full of riddles . . ." I thought to myself.

India? The answer was very simple. Aristarkh Platonovich

was at present in India, hence Strizh's threat to send a registered letter to "India." As for the "changing room," that was an actors' joke. It was the nickname they had given—and it had stuck—to the anteroom to the main directors' office, where Polixena Vasilievna worked. She was Aristarkh Platonovich's secretary.

"And Augusta Avdeyevna?"

"She is Ivan Vasilievich's secretary, of course."

"Aha, aha."

"You may aha if you like," said Bombardov, looking thoughtfully at me, "but I strongly advise you to make as good an impression as you can on Toropetzkaya."

"But I'm no good at doing that!"

"Well you must try, all the same."

Clutching my rolled-up manuscript I climbed toward the upper reaches of the theater and reached the place where I had been told I should find the "changing room."

Outside it there was a sort of lobby with a sofa, where I stopped, feeling nervous, straightened my tie and tried to think of the best way of making a good impression on Polixena Toropetzkaya. I was amazed to hear what sounded like sobbing coming from the changing room. "How odd," I thought and walked in. It was immediately clear that I had not been imagining things. I guessed that the lady with the gorgeous complexion and the scarlet jumper sitting behind a yellow desk was Polixena Toropetzkaya; it was she who was sobbing.

Horrified, unnoticed, I stopped in the doorway.

Tears were running down Toropetzkaya's cheeks; one hand was crumpling a handkerchief, the other was banging the desk top. A thickset, pockmarked man in a green uniform, his eyes swiveling with terror and grief, was standing in front of the desk and stabbing the air with his hands.

"Polixena Vasilievna!" cried the man in a voice wild with despair. "Polixena Vasilievna! They haven't signed it yet! They sign it tomorrow!"

"It's mean!" screamed Polixena Vasilievna. "You've done a mean thing, Demyan Kozmich—mean!"

"Polixena Vasilievna!"

"Those people downstairs have been hatching a plot against Aristarkh Platonovich. They've taken advantage of the fact that he's away in India and you've been helping them!"

"Polixena Vasilievna! No!" cried the man in fearful distress, "How could you! After all he's done for me!"

"I don't want to hear another word!" cried Toropetzkaya. "It's all lies, contemptible lies! They've bribed you!"

At this Demyan Kozmich shouted, "Poli . . . Polixena . . ." and suddenly, like a hound giving tongue, he too burst into a deep, muffled bass sob.

Polixena smashed down her fist, meaning to hit the desk, but instead rammed her hand on to the nib of a pen sticking out of a vase. She uttered a low moan, jumped up from the desk, collapsed into an armchair and began to wave her feet, shod in a pair of foreign slippers with rhinestone buckles.

Demyan Kozmich did not exactly shout but somehow howled from the depths of his body, "Oh Lord! Fetch a doctor!" and galloped out, followed by me, into the lobby.

A minute later there rushed past me a man in a gray suit carrying bandages and a medicine bottle, who disappeared into the changing room. I heard him cry, "My dear! Calm yourself!"

"What's happened?" I whispered to Demyan Kozmich in the lobby.

"Well, you see, sir," boomed Demyan Kozmich turning his desperate, tearful eyes toward me, "I was sent to the commissioner's office to collect the holiday travel warrants for our people to go to the Black Sea in October . . . Well sir, they handed me the four warrants but someone had forgotten to send Aristarkh Platonovich's cousin's name to the commissioner's office so there wasn't one for him . . . All right, they said, you can come and get his warrant at twelve tomorrow . . . And for that, if you please, they say I'm hatching a plot!" It was obvious from Demyan Kozmich's agonized expression that his heart was pure, that he had never hatched a plot and never would in his life.

A faint "Ow!" was heard coming from the changing room

and Demyan Kozmich vanished from the lobby. Ten minutes later the doctor emerged. I sat waiting on the sofa for a while until I heard the sound of the typewriter, then took courage and went in.

Polixena Toropetzkaya, having powdered her face and calmed down, was sitting behind the desk and typing. I bowed, trying to make it a charming but utterly dignified bow and spoke up in a dignified and pleasant voice, although to my consternation the voice that came out sounded strained and false. Explaining who I was, that I had been sent by Strizh to dictate my play to her, I was invited by Polixena to sit down and wait, which I did.

The walls of the changing room were liberally hung with photographs, daguerrotypes and pictures, dominated by a large portrait in oils of an imposing man in a frock coat and sporting the side-whiskers which were fashionable in the seventies. I guessed that this must be Aristarkh Platonovich, but I could not understand who was the ethereal white girl or woman peering out from behind his head and holding a transparent veil. This mystery worried me so much that choosing an appropriate moment I coughed and asked who she was.

There was a pause, during which Polixena fixed her gaze on me as if studying me and finally replied, with slight embarrassment, "That is the muse."

"Aha," I said.

Again the typewriter began to tap. I stared around the walls again and discovered that Aristarkh Platonovich was in every one of the pictures in the company of various other people. Thus a yellowing old photograph showed Aristarkh Platonovich standing at the edge of a wood. He was dressed in town clothes as if for autumn wearing boots, overcoat and top hat. His companion was wearing a short fur-trimmed jacket, a game bag over one shoulder and carrying a double-barreled shotgun. The man's face, his pince-nez and grizzled beard struck me as somewhat familiar.

It was then that Polixena Toropetzkaya exhibited a remarkable charcteristic—an ability to be simultaneously typing and yet aware by some magic of what was happening behind her back. I actually jumped when before I had even asked her she said, "Yes, that's Aristarkh Platonovich out shooting with Turgenev."

In the same way I learned that the two men in fur coats on the steps of the "Slavyansky Bazaar" restaurant, standing beside a two-horse cab, were Aristarkh Platonovich and Ostrovsky.

The four people seated around a table with a fig tree in the background were Aristarkh Platonovich, Pisemsky, Grigorovich and Leskov.

There was no need to ask about the next picture: that barefooted old man in a long peasant shirt, his hands thrust into his belt, eyebrows like bushes, bald but luxuriantly bearded, could be none other than Leo Tolstoi. Facing him stood Aristarkh Platonovich in a flat straw hat and tussore jacket.

But the watercolor next to it amazed me beyond bounds. "It can't be!" I thought. Seated on an armchair in a poorly furnished room was a man with a long birdlike nose, sick and anxious eyes, with hair that fell in straight, lank locks to his sunken cheeks, in pale tight trousers strapped under his square-toed boots and a blue frock coat. There was a manuscript in his hands, a candle in a holder on the table.

The young man of about sixteen, without any side-whiskers but with the same proud nose was unmistakably Aristarkh Platonovich in a short jacket, leaning his arms on the table.

"Yes, that's Gogol reading the second half of *Dead Souls* to Aristarkh Platonovich."

The hairs stood up on the back of my neck as though someone had blown on them from behind and I blurted out involuntarily, "How old is Aristarkh Platonovich then?"

I received a suitable answer to this rude question. As she spoke a sort of vibration could be heard in Polixena's voice, "For such men as Aristarkh Platonovich age has no significance. You are amazed, I suppose, that so many people have been able to enjoy his company during his working life?"

"Oh no, I beg your pardon!" I cried, terrified. "On the

contrary! I . . ." I could find nothing rational to say further because it had suddenly occurred to me—"What do I mean by saying 'on the contrary'? I must be mad!"

Polixena said no more and I thought, "Oh, dear, I obviously haven't made a good impression on her."

The door now opened and a lady bustled into the changing room. One look at her was enough for me to recognize her from the portrait gallery as Ludmilla Silvestrovna Pryakhina. She was exactly like her portrait: the same beret, the same handkerchief held in one hand with the little finger sticking out.

I thought it might do me no harm to try and make a good impression on her too, to kill two birds with one stone as it were, so I gave her a polite bow; but it somehow passed unnoticed.

As she walked in she burst into a carefully modulated laugh and exclaimed, "No, can't you see it? Can't you see it?"

"See what?" asked Toropetzkaya.

"The sun, the sun!" cried Ludmilla Silvestrovna, making great play with her handkerchief and even doing a little dance. "An Indian summer—an Indian summer!"

Polixena gave Ludmilla Silvestrovna an enigmatic stare and said, "You'll have to fill out this questionnaire."

Ludmilla Silvestrovna's gaiety ceased abruptly and her face underwent such a change that I would never have recognized her from her portrait.

"Not another questionnaire? Oh my God, my God!" (Even her voice was unrecognizable now.) "I was just enjoying the sun, concentrating my thoughts, I had just begun to live, the seed was sprouting, the strings were just vibrating, I was walking as into a temple . . . and then . . . Oh, give it here!"

"There's no need to shout, Ludmilla Silvestrovna," remarked Toropetzkaya quietly.

"I'm not shouting! I'm not shouting! I can't read a word, it's so foully printed . . ." Pryakhina glanced down the gray questionnaire form and brusquely pushed it away. "Oh, write it yourself! I don't understand anything about these things!"

Toropetzkaya shrugged her shoulders and picked up a pen.

"My surname's Pryakhina," she said in a nervous screech. "Christian name and patronymic! Ludmilla Silvestrovna! Everybody knows that! I've nothing to hide!"

Toropetzkaya filled in the three words and then asked, "When were you born?"

This question had an astonishing effect on Pryakhina: red spots appeared on her cheekbones and she suddenly said in a whisper, "Holy Mother of God! What is this? Who on earth can want to know that? Why? Why? Well, all right then. I was born in May, in May. What else do they want to know about me?"

"They want to know the *year*," said Toropetzkaya quietly.

Pryakhina's eyes squinted toward her nose and her shoulders started to heave.

"Oh, how I wish," she breathed, "that Ivan Vasilievich could see how you torture an artiste before rehearsal!"

"No, Ludmilla Silvestrovna, you're being impossible," said Toropetzkaya. "Take the questionnaire home and fill it out yourself."

Pryakhina seized the sheet of paper and stuffed it disgustedly into her handbag, her mouth twitching.

The telephone rang and Toropetzkaya barked into the receiver, "Hello! No, comrade! What tickets? No, I haven't any tickets! What? Listen, citizen, you're wasting my time! I haven't got . . . What? Oh!" (Toropetzkaya went red in the face.) "Oh, I'm so sorry! I didn't recognize your voice! Yes, of course, of course! They'll be waiting for you at the box-office! And a program too! I'll personally make sure they keep one for you! And Dmitri Vladimirovich himself won't be coming? Oh, what a shame! What a shame! Yes, yes indeed —goo-o-d-bye!"

In extreme embarrassment Toropetzkaya replaced the receiver and said, "Now thanks to you I've been rude to someone I shouldn't have."

"Oh, forget the whole thing," shrieked Pryakhina, "You've broken the spell, my day has been ruined."

"Oh, by the way," said Toropetzkaya, "the cast manager wants you to go and see him."

A faint pink flush spread over Pryakhina's cheeks and she raised her eyebrows haughtily.

"Why should he want to see me? That's extremely interesting!"

"Mrs. Korolkova the wardrobe mistress has been complaining about you."

"Korolkova, Korolkova?" exclaimed Pryakhina. "Who is she? Ah yes, I remember. And I'm not likely to forget her." Here Ludmilla Silvestrovna gave a laugh which sent a cold shiver down my back, a laugh entirely on the vowel "oo" without opening her lips. "I'm not likely to forget that woman for the way she ruined the hem of my dress. So she's been whining to the manager about me, has she?"

"She is complaining that out of malice you pinched her, in the dressing room, in front of the hairdressers," said Toropetzkaya in a silken voice, a twinkle flashing for a moment in her crystalline eyes.

The effect produced by Toropetzkaya's words amazed me. Suddenly Pryakhina opened her mouth wide as though she were at the dentist and two streams of tears spurted from her eyes. I flinched in my chair and involuntarily pulled my legs up. Toropetzkaya pressed a bell. At once Demyan Kozmich's head appeared around the door and as instantly vanished.

Pryakhina meanwhile laid her fist to her forehead and screamed in a high, sharp voice, "They're murdering me! Lord God! Oh, Lord God! Lord God! Holy Mother, look what they're doing to me in this theater! Gerasim Nikolayevich is a traitor! I suppose he's been telling tales about me to Ivan Vasilievich! But I shall throw myself at his feet! I shall implore him to hear me out! . . ." Her voice cracked and dried up.

The door was flung open and the same doctor rushed in holding a vial and a tumbler. Without bothering to inquire what was happening he poured some cloudy liquid from the vial into the tumbler with a practiced gesture, but Pryakhina screamed hoarsely, "Leave me alone! Leave me alone! Oh, you horrible people!" and ran out.

The doctor tore out after her, crying "My dear! My dear!"

and behind the doctor, waddling along on his gouty legs, went Demyan Kozmich.

Through the open door came the tinkle of a piano and a distant, powerful voice rose in passionate song, ". . . and thou shalt be-e-e the queen of . . ." with a triumphant flourish . . . "the wo-o-rld!" Then the door slammed and the voice was cut off.

"Well, I'm free now. Shall we begin?" said Toropetzkaya, with a charming smile.

CHAPTER ELEVEN

I DISCOVER
THE THEATER

T O R O P E T Z K A Y A was an ideal exponent of the art of typewriting. I have never seen anything like it. There was no need to dictate punctuation to her, nor to repeat the character's name at the beginning of each new piece of dialogue. I reached the point where, pacing up and down the changing room and dictating, I would stop, reflect, then say, "No, wait . . ." and change the text. I completely forgot to indicate which character was speaking, I muttered, I talked aloud, but whatever I did Toropetzkaya produced page after page that needed practically no corrections and without a single grammatical error—copy clean enough, in fact, to hand straight to the printer.

We worked to a continual accompaniment of telephone

calls. At first they disturbed me, but after a while I grew so used to them that I actually enjoyed them. Polixena dealt with callers with extraordinary dexterity. She would exclaim, "Hello, yes. Speak up, comrade, I'm busy. What is it?"

This method invariably reduced the comrade on the other end of the wire to confusion; he would stutter some nonsense and Polixena would swiftly cut him short.

Toropetzkaya's field of competence was extremely wide, as I could observe from the telephone calls.

"Hello!" she would say: "No, this is the wrong extension. I haven't got any tickets . . . 'I'll shoot you!' " (this to me, repeating the last sentence of dialogue which she had typed).

Another ring.

"All tickets sold out," said Toropetzkaya, "and I've no more passes . . . 'That proves nothing!' " (to me).

"I'm now beginning to realize," I thought, "how many people there are in Moscow trying to get a free seat at the theater. And the odd thing is that none of them would think of trying to take a free streetcar ride and none of them would ever go into a shop and ask for a free tin of sardines. Why on earth do they imagine they don't have to pay for a theater ticket?"

"Hello, yes!" shouted Toropetzkaya into the telephone, "Calcutta, the Punjab, Madras, Allahabad . . . No, we can't give his address . . . Yes?" she turned to me.

" 'I won't allow him to go and sing Spanish serenades under my fiancée's window,' " I recited feverishly as I paced the changing room.

" 'Fiancée's window . . .' " Toropetzkaya repeated.

Regularly every minute the little bell on the typewriter would give a "ping" and then the telephone would ring again.

"Hello! Independent Theater! No, I have no tickets! 'Fiancée's window . . .' "

" 'Window!' " I said. " 'Yermakov drops his guitar to the floor and runs out onto the balcony.' "

"Hello? Independent! No, I haven't any tickets! 'Balcony . . .' "

" 'Anna rushes . . .' No, simply 'goes out after him.' "

" 'Goes out . . .' Hello? Oh, yes. Comrade Butovich, your tickets will be waiting for you at the box office. Goodbye."

" 'Anna: He's going to shoot himself.

"Bakhtin: No, he won't!' "

"Hello! Oh, hello, how are you? Yes, with her. Then they go to the Andaman Islands. I'm afraid I can't give any addresses, Albert Albertovich . . . 'No, he won't!' "

To give Polixena her due, she knew her job. She typed busily, and as soon as the telephone rang she would type with one hand, pick up the receiver with the other and shout, "He didn't like Calcutta, but he's feeling very well . . ."

Demyan Kozmich came in frequently to hand bits of paper over the desk. With her right eye Toropetzkaya read them, rubber-stamped them with her right hand while continuing to type with her left: " 'An accordion plays a gay tune, but . . .' "

"No, wait, wait," I exclaimed, "no, no 'gay,' perhaps 'with bravura' . . . or no, wait . . ." I stared wildly at the walls, not having the slightest idea how an accordion played.

Toropetzkaya utilized the pause to powder her nose and tell some woman on the telephone that Albert Albertovich was going to get the corset stays in Vienna. Various people appeared in the changing room and at first I felt ashamed at dictating in front of them; it was as though I were the only naked person among a crowd of people fully dressed, but I soon got used to it.

Misha Panin frequently came in and out and each time he passed he gave me an encouraging squeeze on the shoulder before going through the door, behind which, I realized, was his office.

A gloomy elderly man came in, sat down in an armchair and glanced through the newspaper. This made him even gloomier and he went out again.

Another visitor was a clean-shaven man with a decadent Roman profile and a pettishly jutting underlip; this was the senior producer, Ivan Alexandrovich Poltoratzky.

"*Mille pardons!* Are you on the second act already? How splendid!" he exclaimed as he passed through the other door, mincing comically to show how hard he was trying not to make a noise.

Whenever the inner office door opened he could be heard talking on the telephone, "I don't care . . . I'm quite unprejudiced . . . It's an original idea to have them come running on stage in their underpants. But India wouldn't accept it . . . He's had all the characters fitted with identical long underpants—the prince, the husband *and* the baron—all in the same color? . . . Well, you tell him that they've got to wear trousers. I don't care—get them changed! And tell him to go to hell! Tell him he's talking rot! Petya Dietrich couldn't design costumes like that? Well, he's designed the trousers—I've got the sketches on my desk! Petya . . . He may be outré, but he wears trousers himself! He knows what he's doing!"

In the heat of the day, when I was tearing my hair and trying to think how to express more precisely how a man would fall . . . drop his revolver . . . blood flowing—but *would* it be flowing or not? . . . in came a young, modestly dressed actress and cried, "Dear Polixena Vasilievna—how are you? Look, I've brought you some flowers!"

She kissed Polixena and put four yellow asters on the desk.

"Is there anything about me from India?"

Polixena replied that there was and took out a thick envelope from under the desk. The actress showed great excitement.

" 'Tell Veshnyakova,' " Toropetzkaya read out, " 'that I have solved the problem of the part of Xenia . . .' "

"Ah, yes, yes . . . !" cried Veshnyakova.

" 'I was standing with Praskovya Fryodorovna on the bank of the Ganges and it came to me: the answer is that Veshnyakova should not enter through the big double doors center stage, but from the side, near the piano. She shouldn't forget that she has recently lost her husband and in her state of mind nothing would induce her to come in by the center doors. She should walk like a nun, looking down at the floor and holding a little bunch of marguerites—so appropriate for a widow . . .' "

"God, how true! How profound!" cried Veshnyakova. "It's true! Somehow I felt wrong coming through the big doors . . ."

"Wait a moment," Toropetzkaya went on, "there's some more," and she read on: " 'However, let Veshnyakova use whatever entrance she likes. When I return I will explain exactly what I mean and then it will all be quite clear. I did not care for the Ganges. It is a river, I feel, which lacks something . . .' This doesn't concern you," said Polixena.

"Polixena Vasilievna," said Veshnyakova, "write to Aristarkh Platonovich and tell him that I'm madly, but madly grateful to him!"

"All right."

"Couldn't I write myself?"

"No," replied Polixena, "he said expressly that no one was to write to him except me. It would exhaust him while he is meditating."

"I understand, I understand," cried Veshnyakova and with a kiss for Polixena she departed.

In came a fat, energetic, middle-aged man who beamed as he shouted while still in the doorway:

"Have you heard the latest story? Ah, you're working?"

"That's all right, we're just having a break," said Toropetzkaya and the fat man, visibly bursting to tell his story, shining with joy, leaned toward her and beckoned in all directions to summon an audience. Misha Panin, Poltoratzky and one other gathered around to listen, their heads clustered together over the desk. All I could hear was ". . . and at that moment the husband came back to the hotel . . ." Laughter across the desk. The fat man whispered a little more, at which Misha Panin was seized by a spasm of his special laughter "Ah, ah, ah . . ." Poltoratzky exclaimed: "How splendid!" and the fat man, laughing happily, rushed away shouting, "Vasya! Vasya! Stop! Have you heard? I'm telling a new story!"

But he never managed to tell his story to Vasya because Toropetzkaya called him back.

Aristarkh Platonovich had apparently had something to say about the fat man, too, in his letter.

" 'Tell Yelagin,' " Toropetzkaya read out, " 'that he must do all he can to avoid playing for effect, which he's very much inclined to do.' "

Yelagin's expression changed and he glanced at the letter.

" 'Tell him,' " Toropetzkaya went on, " 'that in the scene at the general's party he shouldn't greet the colonel's wife at once but he should walk around the table first, with an embarrassed smile. He owns a distillery and a man in his position would never march in and straightaway greet a senior officer's wife; but . . .' "

"I don't understand," said Yelagin, "I'm sorry, but I don't understand." Yelagin circled around the room, as if walking around something. "No, it doesn't feel right to me. It feels awkward! . . . There's the colonel's wife standing right in front of him and he makes a detour . . . I feel not, somehow!"

"Do you mean to say that you understand the scene better than Aristarkh Platonovich?" asked Toropetzkaya in an icy voice.

The question upset Yelagin.

"No, I'm not saying that." He blushed. "But look . . ." And he made another circling movement around the room.

"I think you should go down on bended knee and thank Aristarkh Platonovich for writing all the way from India . . ."

"You're always telling people to get down on their knees . . ." Yelagin suddenly grumbled.

"The fellow's got spirit," I thought.

"You'd better listen to the rest of what Aristarkh Platonovich has to say." And she read on: " 'However, let him play it how he likes. I'll explain what I think about the play when I'm back.' "

Yelagin cheered up at this and then did a marvelously funny turn: he drew his hand down one cheek and then down the other and I felt I could actually see him sprouting side-whiskers. He seemed to grow shorter, set his nostrils flaring haughtily and as he plucked a few imaginary hairs out of his imaginary side-whiskers he recited through his clenched teeth everything that had been written about him in the letter.

"What an actor!" I thought. I could see that he was imitating Aristarkh Platonovich.

The blood rushed to Toropetzkaya's face and she started to breathe heavily.

"I beg your pardon . . . !"

"However . . ." said Yelagin through his teeth, then shrugged his shoulders and said in his ordinary voice: "I don't understand it!" and went out. In the lobby I saw him make another circle, shrug his shoulders in bewilderment and disappear.

"Oh, these mediocrities," said Polixena. "Nothing's sacred to them. Have you ever heard them talking among themselves?"

"H'mm," I replied, not knowing what to say and above all not understanding what the word "mediocrities" was supposed to mean.

By the end of the first day it became obvious that it was hopeless to attempt to transcribe the whole play in the changing room. Polixena was released from her usual duties for two days and she and I moved into one of the ladies' dressing rooms. Panting, Demyan Kozmich carried the typewriter there for us.

The Indian summer faded and gave way to a wet autumn. Gray light filtered in through the window. I sat on a little couch, reflected in the wardrobe mirror, and Polixena sat on a stool. I felt as though my mind existed on two stories. On the upper floor was chaos and confusion, which had to be reduced to order. The heroes of my play were so demanding that they caused me a great deal of mental agony. Each one wanted the right words to say, each one tried to play the lead and push the others aside. Steering the play in the right direction was extremely exhausting work. The upper story of my head was full of noise and movement and prevented me from enjoying the calm and tidiness which reigned in the lower story. Women with exaggeratedly ripe lips and shadows under their eyes, smiling artificial smiles, gazed down on me from the walls of the little dressing room, so small that it was no bigger than a shoe box. The women were all wearing crinolines or farthingales. Behind them, flashing their teeth for the photographer, stood various men carrying top hats. One of them was in uniform with heavy epaulettes. A fat drunkard's nose hung down almost to his upper lips, his cheeks and neck were creased into folds. I wouldn't have recognized him as the actor Galin if Polixena hadn't told me who it was.

I stared at the photographs, got up, touched the bare, unlit electric lamps, the empty powder bowl, breathed in the barely perceptible smell of make-up and the aroma of Polixena's cigarettes. It was quiet here, the silence only broken by the clicking of the typewriter, the subdued tinkle of its little bell and an occasional creak from the parquet floor. Through the open door I caught a glimpse now and then of some rather desiccated-looking elderly women who walked past on tiptoe carrying heaps of starched petticoats.

Occasionally the deep silence of the passage would be broken by muffled snatches of music and fearful distant shrieks. On stage, somewhere deep within that labyrinth of old corridors, ramps and staircases they were rehearsing *Stenka Razin*.

We started transcribing at noon and at two o'clock we took a break. Polixena went home to do her housework and I went along to the buffet. To reach it I had to leave the corridor and go down some stairs. Here the enchanted silence was loudly disturbed. Actors and actresses were walking up the staircase; a telephone was ringing behind some white doors, while the answering peal of another telephone was heard from below. Downstairs one of the messengers under Augusta Menazhraki's tutelage was sitting on duty. Then—a medieval-looking iron door, beyond it some mysterious steps and a sort of brick-walled canyon, limitless in height or so it seemed to me, solemn, sunk in semiobscurity. Leaning against the walls of this ravine stood layers of scenery. I could just make out strange cryptic inscriptions on their white framework—!"1st left rear," "Count, back," "Bedroom, Act III." To the right was a pair of vast, tall, time-blackened doors, pierced by a wicket gate with a monstrous padlock. These, I discovered, led onto the stage. There was a similar pair of doors to the left, which opened into the courtyard and through which the workmen brought in from outdoor sheds those pieces of scenery which were not stored in the scenery dock. I always used to dawdle in that great canyon whenever I wanted to daydream alone; it was easy to do so because hardly anyone ever walked down the narrow pathway between the stacks of scenery. When they did, one had to turn round and press oneself flat to allow them to pass.

With a sigh like the soft hiss of a serpent the pneumatic spring on the iron door let me out. My feet no longer made a sound as I walked along the carpet, I recognized the ante-room to Gavriil Stepanovich's office by its eagle's-head door handle and I passed along the broadcloth carpeting toward the spot where I could just see and hear a crowd of people—the buffet.

The first thing to meet the eye behind the counter was a gleaming samovar of several gallons' capacity and after that a short, elderly man with drooping moustaches, a bald head and such sad eyes that until one got used to him, everyone who saw him was seized with pity and anxiety. Sighing wistfully, the sad man stood behind the counter staring at the pile of bread and butter slices spread with red caviar and sheep's-milk cheese. The actors would come up to the counter to collect their food and the buffet-attendant's eyes would fill with tears. He gained no cheer from the money they paid for his sandwiches, not from the knowledge that he was working in the best place in the whole city, the Independent Theater. Nothing cheered him and obviously he suffered agonies at the thought that everything on the plate would be devoured to the last morsel and that the entire contents of that gigantic samovar was doomed to be drunk.

The light of a lachrymose autumn day came in through the two windows, on the wall behind the buffet counter a gas mantle glowed steadily; the corners of the room swam in perpetual twilight.

I felt shy at so many strangers seated at the tables and was afraid to go and join any of them, although I longed to. Muffled laughter came from the tables and everywhere people were holding forth or telling stories.

After drinking my glass of tea and eating a slice of bread and cheese I explored other parts of the theater. My favorite was the place known as "the office." It was quite different from anywhere else in the theater because it was the only place that was noisy; it was the point where life, as it were, gushed in from the street.

The office consisted of two parts: the first was a little narrow room reached from out-of-doors by a flight of steps, built on purpose in exactly the way to make strangers to the theater trip. In this little anteroom sat two messengers, Katkov and Bakvalin. In front of them on a little table were two telephones and these telephones rang almost without cease.

I very soon realized that the callers on both telephones were all telephoning one and the same man and that this man was installed in the adjacent room, on the door to which hung a notice:

HOUSE MANAGER
PHILIPP PHILIPPOVICH TULUMBASOV

In all Moscow there never was and probably never will be a more popular man than Tulumbasov. The entire city, it seemed, was struggling to telephone Tulumbasov and first Katkov and then Bakvalin would connect Philipp Philippovich with his important callers.

I can't remember whether I was told or whether I imagined it, but Julius Caesar is supposed to have been able to do several things at once, such as read and listen at the same time. I hereby declare that Julius Caesar would have been hopelessly lost if he had been given Philipp Philippovich's job to do. Apart from the two telephones which pealed away in front of Bakvalin and Katkov there were two more **on Philipp**

Philippovich's own desk and one of the old-fashioned sort fixed to the wall.

Philipp Philippovich, a pleasant fair-haired man with a kindly round face, had exceptionally alert eyes behind which lurked a barely perceptible, secret, ineradicable sadness. He sat behind a barrier in a well-appointed corner of his office. Day or night outside, in Philipp's office it was always evening and the green-shaded lamp always burned. On the desk in front of him were four calendars, marked all over with mysterious signs like: "Pryakh. 2, seats 4," "13 mat. 2," "Mon. 77727" and so on. Similar hieroglyphics were scribbled in five open notebooks on the desk. Behind Philipp reared a stuffed brown bear with electric bulbs in its eyes. At any hour of the day people in the most extraordinary variety of clothes were to be found leaning on their stomachs across Philipp's barrier. It would be no exaggeration to say that the whole of Russia passed in front of Philipp Philippovich. His office was the meeting point of all classes, groups, strata, persuasions, sexes, ages. Poorly dressed old women in ragged hats would be followed by soldiers with arm-of-service tabs of every color; the soldiers would give way to well-dressed men with beaver-trimmed coats and starched collars. Among the starched collars there would be an occasional Russian side-buttoned shirt. A cloth cap on a mop of curls. A *dame de luxe* with an ermine wrap. A fur hat with ear flaps, a black eye. A young creature of the female sex with a powdered nose. A man in waders and a jerkin belted with a piece of rope. Another soldier, a one-striper. A clean-shaven man with a bandaged head. An old woman with a quivering jaw and deathly eyes, talking French to her lady companion, who was wearing men's galoshes. A sheepskin coat.

Those who could not lean on the barrier crowded in from behind, now and again waving crumpled pieces of paper or calling timidly, "Philipp Philippovich!" Occasionally men or women without overcoats wearing only jackets or blouses would wriggle their way into the crowd besieging the barrier; these, I realized, were actresses and actors of the Independent Theater. No matter who it was who got as far as the barrier, each one without exception wore a look of cunning or an ingratiating smile. Everybody there wanted something from Philipp Philippovich; everybody depended on his reply.

The three telephones rang incessantly and sometimes the little office was deafened by all three ringing at once. None of this disturbed Philipp in the least. With his right hand he picked up the receiver of the right-hand telephone, clamped it between his shoulder and his cheek, with his left hand he picked up the other receiver and pressed it to his left ear. Freeing his right hand he used it to take one of the notes being handed to him and began talking to three people at once—into the left-hand telephone, the right-hand and then the visitor again. Right-hand telephone, visitor, left, left, right, right. Dropping both receivers back onto their rests at once and thus freeing both hands, he took two of the scraps of paper. Refusing one of them, he picked up the receiver from the yellow telephone, listened for a moment and said: "Call tomorrow at three o'clock." He hung up and said to the petitioner, "Nothing doing."

In time I began to understand what they wanted from Philipp Philippovich. They wanted tickets.

They begged for tickets in every conceivable way. There were some who said that they had come all the way from Irkutsk, were going back that night and couldn't possibly leave without seeing *The Girl Without a Dowry*. Someone would say that he was in charge of an excursion from Yalta, or the representative of some delegation. Someone else who wasn't a tourist guide, who wasn't a Siberian and wasn't going away anywhere might simply say, "My name's Petukhov —remember?"

Actresses and actors said, "Phil, oh Phil, fix it, will you?"

Someone said, "At any price, I don't care what it costs . . ."

"Having known Ivan Vasilievich for twenty-eight years," mumbled an old woman in a moth-eaten beret, "I'm sure he wouldn't refuse me . . ."

"You can have a standing place," said Philipp suddenly

and before the astounded old woman could say anything more he handed her a piece of paper.

"There are eight of us . . ." began a powerfully-built man; the rest of his speech died on his lips, as Phil was already saying, "Free seats,"—and handing him a chit.

"I've come from Arnold Arnoldovich," said a smartly-dressed young man.

"Standing place," I mentally prompted, but I was wrong.

"Nothing doing, sir," rapped out Phil, after a single glance at the young man's face.

"But Arnold . . ."

"Nothing doing!"

And the young man vanished as though swallowed up by the ground.

"My wife and I . . ." began a fat citizen.

"For tomorrow?" said Phil rapidly and jerkily.

"Very well."

"At the box office!" said Phil and the fat man pushed his way out holding a scrap of paper, by which time Phil was already barking into the telephone: "No! Tomorrow!" whilst simultaneously reading a proffered note with his left eye.

In time I realized that he was never guided by people's outward appearance, any more than he was by their greasy bits of paper. There were people who were modestly, even poorly dressed who to my amazement were suddenly given two free tickets in the fourth row and there were some well-dressed ones who went out empty-handed. People brought huge red travel-warrants from Astrakhan, Eupatoria, Vologda or Leningrad and none of them had any effect, or would only be effective in five days' time; sometimes shy, silent people would come who never said anything but simply stretched their hand across the barrier and immediately got a ticket.

Growing wiser as I watched I could see that in front of me was a man with a perfect knowledge of human nature. This realization thrilled me. I was faced by a psychologist of the highest order. He saw into the innermost depths of people's souls. He guessed their secret desires; their passions, their sins were an open book to him, he knew everything that was concealed within them, good as well as evil. And above all he knew their rights. He knew who should come to the theater and when, who had the right to sit in the fourth row and who must crowd into the gallery and sit on the steps of the aisle in the wild hope that somehow, someone might magically give up their seat.

How could Philipp have failed to understand his fellow creatures so well when tens of thousands of people had passed before him in his fifteen years of service? They included engineers, surgeons, actors, presidents of women's clubs, embezzlers, housewives, lathe operators, teachers, mezzosopranos, builders, guitarists, pickpockets, experts on Dante, firemen, young ladies of no fixed occupation, photographers, planners, pilots, Pushkin scholars, collective-farm chairmen, cocottes, jockeys, fitters, department-store salesgirls, students, hairdressers, steel erectors, former landlords, pensioners, village schoolmasters, vintners, cellists, conjurors, divorcées, café managers, poker players, homeopaths, accompanists, graphomaniacs, ticket checkers from the conservatoire, chemists, conductors, athletes, chess players, laboratory assistants, tramps, bookkeepers, schizophrenics, food tasters, manicurists, accountants, unfrocked priests, black marketeers.

Why did Philipp need those slips of paper?

One look and the first few words from anyone who appeared in front of him were enough for him to know their due, and Philipp Philippovich's answers were always right.

"Yesterday," said an agitated woman, "I bought two tickets for *Don Carlos*, put them in my handbag, and when I got home . . ."

But Philipp had already pressed a buzzer and without another glance at the woman said, "Bakvalin! Two lost tickets . . . row?"

"Elev . . ."

"In row eleven. Let her in and give her two seats. Check it!"

"Very good," growled Bakvalin and the lady was gone; someone else was already leaning over the barrier and squeaking that he was leaving Moscow tomorrow.

"You can't do that!" exclaimed an angry woman, her eyes flashing. "He's over sixteen! Just because he's wearing shorts . . ."

"We do not concern ourselves, madam, with the length of people's trousers," replied Philipp in a metallic voice, "by law children under fifteen are not admitted. Sit down a moment, I'll be with you . . ." he said simultaneously in intimate tones to a clean-shaven actor.

"Look here," shouted the scandalized woman, "you've just let in three young boys in long trousers. I shall complain!"

"Those boys, madam," answered Phil, "were midgets from Kostroma."

There was absolute silence. The lady's face fell and Phil gave her a smile which made her shudder. The people jostling each other at the barrier giggled maliciously.

A pale-faced actor, his eyes clouded with pain, suddenly lurched sideways against the barrier, muttering, "Ghastly migraine . . ."

Quite unmoved, Phil stretched his hand out behind him without turning around, opened a wall cabinet, groped for a box, took a little packet from it, handed it to the sufferer and said, "Drink that with some water . . . Yes, madam . . ."

The woman was weeping, her hat had slipped down over her ear. She was greatly upset and was wiping her nose with a dirty handkerchief. Yesterday, apparently, she too had bought tickets for *Don Carlos*, had gone home and found that her handbag had disappeared. It had contained a hundred and seventy-five rubles, a powder puff and a handkerchief.

"That's bad," said Phil sternly. "You should keep your money in the savings bank and not in your handbag."

The woman goggled at Phil, shocked by such an unsympathetic reaction to her misfortune. Phil immediately pulled out the squeaky drawer of his desk and a moment later a battered handbag adorned with a yellowing metal seashell was in the woman's hand. She mumbled her gratitude.

"The body's arrived, Philipp Philippovich," announced Bakvalin.

At once the light was turned off, the desk drawers were shut with a creak, and pulling on his overcoat Phil pushed his way through the crowd and out. As though spellbound, I followed him; hitting my head against the wall at the turn of the staircase, I emerged into the yard. Outside the office door stood a hearse, swathed in red bunting and on the hearse, gazing up into the autumn sky with closed eyes, lay a fireman. His helmet glittered at his feet and his head was wreathed in fir branches. Hatless, Phil stood beside the hearse with a solemn face, giving silent orders to Kushov, Bakvalin and Klyukvin. The hearse hooted and moved out into the street. A fanfare of several trombones rang out. Vaguely bewildered, passersby stopped and the hearse halted. A bearded man in an overcoat could be seen on the steps of the theater waving a conductor's baton. Obedient to it, a small, shining brass band deafened the street. The music stopped as suddenly as it had begun. The golden trumpet bells and the conductor's red goatee both disappeared up the steps. Kuskov jumped onto the hearse, three firemen took up their places at the corners of the coffin. With a farewell gesture from Phil the hearse set off for the crematorium and Phil returned to the office.

The life of a great city pulses in waves—there is always an ebb and flow. Now and again the wave of Phil's applicants would slacken without any apparent reason and Phil would allow himself to lean back in an armchair, joke, relax.

"I've been sent to see you," said an actor from some other theater.

"They've picked a real scoundrel to send," replied Phil, smiling with his cheek muscles only. (Phil's eyes never smiled.)

Through Phil's door there now entered a very pretty woman in a magnificently cut overcoat and a dark-brown fox fur over her shoulders. Phil gave a welcoming smile and cried, "*Bonjour*, Missy!"

The lady smiled in reply. Behind her there came dawdling into the office a seven-year-old boy in a sailor-suit, with a haughty look on his face which was smeared with chocolate, and with three scratch marks under his eyes. The boy was quietly hiccupping at regular intervals and was followed by a fat, worried woman.

"Pfui, Alyosha!" she exclaimed with a German accent.

"Hello, young man," said Phil, offering his hand to the boy, who hiccupped, bowed and shuffled his feet.

"Pfui, Alyosha," whispered Amalia Ivanovna.

"Amalia Ivanovna!" said the boy quietly and threateningly, covertly shaking his fist at Amalia Ivanovna.

"Pfui, Alyosha," said Amalia Ivanovna softly.

"What's that under your eye?" asked Phil.

"I," whispered the boy, with a hiccup, "had a fight with George . . ."

"Pfui, Alyosha," whispered Amalia Ivanovna, automatically mouthing the words with her lips only.

"*C'est dommage!*" bellowed Phil and produced a bar of chocolate from his desk drawer.

"Alyosha, you haff eat fourteen today," whispered Amalia Ivanovna timidly.

"Don't tell lies, Amalia Ivanovna," squeaked the boy, imagining that he was whispering.

"Pfui, Alyosha!"

"Phil, you've completely forgotten about me, you horrible man!" exclaimed the lady.

"*Non, madam, impossible!*" cried Phil. "*Mais les affaires toujours!*"

With a rippling laugh the lady slapped Phil on the hand with her glove.

"I know what!" she said, seized with inspiration, "My Darya has baked some pies today—come and have dinner with me."

"*Avec plaisir!*" exclaimed Phil and in the lady's honor he lit the eyes of the bear.

"How you frightened me, Phil, you horrid creature!" she cried.

"Alyosha, look at the bear . . . just as if it vos alive!" said Amalia Ivanovna in a burst of artificial enthusiasm.

"Let me through!" roared the boy and pushed forward toward the barrier.

"Pfui, Alyosha . . ."

"Bring Argunin with you," exclaimed the lady as though struck by a sudden brainwave.

"*Il joue!*"

"Well, he can come after the show," said the lady, turning her back on Amalia Ivanovna.

"*Je transporte lui.*"

"All right, my dear, then that's settled. Yes, Phil dear, I've a favor to ask you. Couldn't you find a seat somewhere for an old lady for *Don Carlos?* Mm? In the dress circle, maybe? Could you, dear?"

"Your dressmaker?" asked Phil, looking at her with his all-comprehending eyes.

"You are beastly!" exclaimed the lady. "Why do you think she's my dressmaker? She's the widow of a professor and now . . ."

"She dressmakes," said Phil as if in a dream, writing in his notebook: "Byeloshvei. Mi. back d.-circle. 13th."

"How did you guess her name?" exclaimed the lady, blushing prettily.

"Philipp Philippovich, the manager wants you on the telephone," shouted Bakvalin.

"Just coming!"

"While you're talking I'll call my husband," said the lady.

As Phil bounded out of the room the lady picked up the receiver and dialed a number.

"Director's office, please. How are you, my dear? I've asked Phil to come and eat pies with us this evening. Well, that's all right, you can take a nap for an hour or so. Oh, and I've invited Argunin too . . . I can't discuss that here . . . Goodbye, my dear . . . Why do you sound so worried? There's a kiss for you."

Leaning on the checkered back of the couch and closing my eyes I was daydreaming: "Oh, what a world . . . a world of calm and pleasure . . ." I pictured the unknown lady's apartment. For some reason I imagined it as being enormous, a picture in a gold frame hung on the wall of the vast hallway, the parquet gleamed, in the drawing room was a grand piano, a huge carpet . . .

My reverie was suddenly rudely broken off by a low groan and intestinal rumblings. I opened my eyes.

The boy, deathly pale, rolling his eyes, was sitting on the couch with his feet spread wide on the floor. The lady and Amalia Ivanovna were leaning over him. The lady had grown pale.

"Alyosha!" she cried. "What's the matter?"

"Pfui, Alyosha! What's the matter with you?" exclaimed Amalia Ivanovna.

"I've got a headache," replied the child in a weak, trembling baritone and his cap fell over his eyes. He suddenly blew out his cheeks and turned even paler.

"Oh, my God!" shrieked the lady.

A few minutes later an open taxicab drew up in the courtyard with Bakvalin standing on the running board.

Wiping the boy's mouth with a handkerchief they led him out of the office.

Oh, that glorious world of the office! Phil—farewell! Soon I shall be gone forever. Think of me sometimes!

CHAPTER TWELVE

SIVTSEV VRAZHEK

I DID NOT even notice that Toropetzkaya and I had finished transcribing the script. Nor had I time to reflect on what might happen next, before fate itself prompted the next move.

Klyukvin brought me a letter.

MY DEAR LEONTII SERGEYEVICH

Why in heaven's name does he think I'm called Leontii Sergeyevich? Probably because it's easier to pronounce than Sergei Lontievich. Anyhow, who cares?

. . . You must read your play to Ivan Vasilievich. Go to Sivtsev Vrazhek on Monday the 13th at twelve noon.

Yours sincerely,
THOMAS STRIZH

I was very thrilled, as I realized the exceptional importance of this letter. I decided to wear a starched collar, a light blue tie and a gray suit. It was not difficult to decide on the latter, as the gray one was the only decent suit I possessed. I would behave politely but with dignity and—God forbid—without a hint of servility. The thirteenth, as I well remember, was the following day and in the morning I saw Bombardov at the theater. His advice struck me as curious in the extreme.

"As you pass a big gray house," said Bombardov, "you turn left into a little cul-de-sac. From there you'll find it easily. Wrought iron gates and a colonnade along the front of the house. There's no entrance from the street, so you must turn the corner and go in through the courtyard. There you'll see a man in a sheepskin coat who will ask you, 'What do you want?' and you must reply with a single word, 'Appointment.'"

"Is that the password?" I asked. "What if the man's not there?"

"He'll be there," said Bombardov and went on coldly, "In the corner, opposite the man in the sheepskin coat you'll see a jacked-up automobile without any wheels, beside it a bucket and a man washing the car."

"Have you been there today?" I asked in amazement.

"I was there a month ago."

"Then how do you know that there'll be a man washing a car?"

"Because he takes the wheels off and washes it every day."

"But doesn't Ivan Vasilievich drive in it sometimes?"

"He never drives in it."

"Why not?"

"Where would he go?"

"Well, to the theater, for instance?"

"Ivan Vasilievich drives to the theater twice a year for dress rehearsals and then they hire Drykin's coach."

"How extraordinary! Why hire a coach when he's got a car?"

"And if the chauffeur dies of a heart attack at the wheel

and the car drives into a shop window, what happens then, might I ask?"

"But supposing the horse bolts?"

"Drykin's horse never bolts. It never goes faster than a walk. Opposite the man with the bucket there's a door. You will go in and walk up a wooden staircase. Then there's another door. Go in. There you'll see a black bust of Ostrovsky. Opposite it are some little white columns and a black, black stove. Squatting beside it and stoking it will be a man in felt boots."

I burst into laughter, "Are you quite sure that he'll be there and actually squatting?"

"Absolutely," replied Bombardov drily with a straight face.

"It will be interesting to see if you're right!"

"Try it and see. He will ask you anxiously: 'Where are you going?' and you will reply . . ."

"Appointment?"

"Mm'hm. Then he'll say to you: 'Take off your coat here, please.' You'll find yourself in the hall and a nurse will meet you and ask: 'What have you come for?' and you will reply . . ."

I nodded.

"First of all Ivan Vasilievich will ask you who your father was. What was he?"

"Deputy-governor of a province."

Bombardov frowned.

"Er . . . no, that won't really do. No, no. Say that he worked in a bank."

"I don't like that at all. Why should I start telling lies the moment I see him?"

"Because it might upset him and . . ."

I could only blink.

". . . and it can't matter to you to say he worked in a bank or something like that . . . Then he'll ask what you think of homeopathy. And you'll say that you took a homeopathic remedy for stomach trouble last year and it did you a lot of good."

Just then a bell rang and Bombardov had to hurry off to a

rehearsal, so he gave me the rest of his instructions very briefly.

"You don't know Misha Panin, you were born in Moscow," said Bombardov rapidly, "and if he asks you about Thomas Strizh you must say you don't like him. Whatever he says about your play, don't object. Don't read that bit in Act III where there's a shot . . ."

"How can I avoid reading it when the character shoots himself?"

The bell rang again. Bombardov ran off into the semidarkness, his muffled cry reaching me from the distance, "Don't read about the shot! And you haven't got a cold!"

Completely staggered by Bombardov's puzzling instructions I turned up at the cul-de-sac in Sivtsev Vrazhek a minute before noon.

There was no man in a sheepskin coat in the courtyard, but in his place stood a peasant woman in a headscarf. She asked: "What do you want?" and stared suspiciously at me. The word "appointment" satisfied her completely and I turned the corner. On the precise spot described by Bombardov stood a coffee-colored automobile, but with its wheels on. A man was wiping down the bodywork with a rag. Beside the car was a bucket and a bottle of something.

Following Bombardov's directions I found my way unerringly and reached the bust of Ostrovsky. "Oho," I thought, remembering Bombardov: although some birch logs were burning merrily in the stove, there was no sign of anyone squatting beside it; but before I had time to laugh an old, dark, varnished oak door opened and through it came a little old man carrying a shovel and wearing patched felt boots. Catching sight of me he looked startled and blinked.

"What do you want, citizen?" he asked.

"Appointment," I replied, reveling in the power of the magic word.

The little old man brightened and waved his shovel toward the other door, where an old-fashioned lamp hung from the ceiling. I took off my coat, stuck my script under my arm and knocked on the door. At once there came the sound of a chain-bolt being withdrawn, then a key was turned in the lock and a woman in nurse's uniform looked out.

"What do you want?" she inquired.

"Appointment," I replied.

The woman moved aside, ushered me in and gave me a searching stare.

"Is it cold outside?" she asked.

"No, the weather's fine, it's an Indian summer," I answered.

"You haven't got a cold, have you?" asked the woman.

I gave a start, remembered Bombardov and said, "No, I haven't."

"Knock on that door over there and go in," said the woman sternly and vanished.

Before knocking on the dark, metal-paneled door I glanced around. A white stove; several enormous cupboards. There was a smell of mint and some other agreeable herb. Utter silence reigned, to be suddenly broken by the hoarse note of a clock. It struck twelve times and then from behind a cupboard a cuckoo cuckooed alarmingly.

I knocked at the door, then gripped the enormous, heavy ring and the door opened into a large bright room.

I was so excited that I noticed almost nothing except the couch on which Ivan Vasilievich was sitting. He was exactly like his portrait, though slightly fresher and younger-looking. His black moustache, only faintly tinged with gray, was beautifully shaped. A lorgnette hung by a gold chain on his chest. Ivan Vasilievich surprised me by his captivating smile.

"Delighted," he said, with the faintest trace of a throaty pronunciation, "do sit down."

I sat down in an armchair.

"What is your name and patronymic?" asked Ivan Vasilievich with a friendly look.

"Sergei Leontievich."

"How nice! Well now, and how *are* you, Sergei Paphnutyevich?" As he gazed at me with a charmingly solicitous expression Ivan Vasilievich drummed his fingers on the table; on it were the stub of a pencil and a glass of water covered, for some reason, with a sheet of paper.

"I'm very well indeed, thank you."

"You haven't got a cold?"

"No."

Ivan Vasilievich gave a sort of groan and asked, "And how is your dear father?"

"My father is dead."

"How terrible," replied Ivan Vasilievich, "and whom did he see? Who looked after him?"

"I can't remember exactly, but it was a professor, I think . . . Professor Yankovsky."

"Useless," rejoined Ivan Vasilievich. "He should have gone to see Professor Pletushkov and all would have been well."

I assumed an expression of regret that he had not consulted Pletushkov.

"Better still would have been . . . h'm, h'm . . . homeopathic medicine," Ivan Vasilievich went on. "It is really extraordinary how much good homeopathy can do . . ." here he gave a passing glance at his glass, "do you believe in homeopathy?"

"Bombardov—you're incredible," I thought and began to say vaguely, "Of course, on the one hand . . . I personally . . . although many people don't believe in it . . ."

"They're wrong!" said Ivan Vasilievich. "Fifteen drops—and all pain ceases." He gave another one of his groans and went on: "And what, Sergei Panphilych, was your dear father?"

"Sergei Leontievich," I said gently.

"A thousand pardons!" exclaimed Ivan Vasilievich. "And what was he?"

"I'm not going to lie," I thought and said, "He ended his civil service career as a deputy-governor."

This news banished the smile from Ivan Vasilievich's face.

"I see, I see, I see," he said in a worried tone, then was silent, drummed on the table and said: "Very well, shall we begin?"

I opened my script, coughed, felt faint, coughed again and began reading.

I read the title, then the long list of the cast and started on the stage directions for Act I: "Lights in the distance, a courtyard powdered with snow, the side door of a house. From it can be heard the strains of *Faust* being played on a piano . . ."

Have you ever had to read a play alone with one other person? It is extremely difficult, I assure you. Now and again I glanced up at Ivan Vasilievich and wiped my forehead with a handkerchief. Ivan Vasilievich sat completely motionless, fixing me with an unwavering stare through his lorgnette. I was extremely upset by the fact that he never once smiled, even though there were quite a few funny lines in the first act. The actors had laughed a lot when they had heard it read and one had laughed till he cried. Ivan Vasilievich not only refrained from laughing but even stopped groaning. Every time I looked up at him I saw the same thing—the lorgnette trained firmly on me and behind it those unblinking eyes. As a result I began to think that my funny lines weren't funny at all.

I reached the end of the first act and started on the second. As I listened in the total silence to the sound of my own monotonous voice it sounded like a deacon reading the litany for the dead.

I was seized with apathy and a desire to close the thick, bound typescript. I felt that Ivan Vasilievich was saying grimly to himself, "Will this ever finish?" My voice grew hoarse and I occasionally cleared my throat with a cough. I read first in a tenor then in a deep bass, twice my voice broke into an unexpected squeak but none of this wrung so much as a smile from either of us.

A slight relief came with the sudden appearance of the woman in white. She entered without a sound and Ivan Vasilievich glanced rapidly at his watch. The woman handed Ivan Vasilievich a tumbler. He drank his medicine, chased it down with water from his glass, covered it with its lid and gave another look at his watch. The woman bowed to Ivan Vasilievich with a deep, old-fashioned Russian bow and marched haughtily out.

"Shall we go on?" said Ivan Vasilievich and I started reading again. From far off came the cry of the cuckoo, then the telephone rang behind the screen.

"Excuse me," said Ivan Vasilievich, "a call from the Institute on a matter of the greatest importance . . . Yes," his voice could be heard from behind the screen, "yes . . . h'm . . . h'm . . . it's the same gang at work. I order you to keep it all in the strictest secrecy. A reliable man will be here this evening and we will work out a plan . . ."

Ivan Vasilievich returned and we reached the end of Scene V. It was at the beginning of Scene VI that the most extraordinary event occurred. I heard a door slam somewhere, then the sound of loud and apparently sham weeping; a door, not the one by which I had entered but one which evidently led into the inner rooms, was flung open and into the room there flew, in a state of Satanic terror, a fat tabby cat. It dashed past me toward a tulle curtain, gripped it with its claws and climbed up. The tulle couldn't bear its weight and immediately began to tear. Still tearing the curtain into strips, the cat climbed to the top and from there it gazed around in frenzy. Ivan Vasilievich dropped his lorgnette as Ludmilla Silvestrovna Pryakhina appeared in the door. The mere sight of her was enough to make the cat climb even higher, but it was stopped by the ceiling. The animal fell from the rounded cornice and clung, numb with terror, to the curtain.

Pryakhina came in with eyes closed, pressing a fistful of damp, crumpled handkerchief to her forehead and holding in her other hand a second lace handkerchief which was dry and clean. Running to the middle of the room she dropped onto one knee, bowed her head and stretched her arm forward like a prisoner surrendering her sword to the victor.

"I shall not move from this spot," cried Pryakhina shrilly, "until you, my teacher, give me protection. Pelikan is a traitor! God sees all, all!"

Just then the tulle gave a ripping sound and an eighteen-inch split opened up above the cat.

"Shoo!" Ivan Vasilievich suddenly shrieked despairingly and clapped his hands.

The cat slithered down the curtain, tearing it all the way and bounded out of the room. Pryakhina started sobbing in a thunderous voice and covering her eyes with her hands she exclaimed, choking with tears, "What do I hear? Do my ears deceive me? Is my teacher and benefactor driving me out? Oh God! Oh God, be my witness!!"

"Look around, Ludmilla Silvestrovna!" cried Ivan Vasilievich in despair.

An old woman now appeared in the doorway and cried:

"Come back, dear—there's a stranger here!"

Ludmilla Silvestrovna opened her eyes and saw my gray suit in the gray armchair. Her eyes bulged at the sight of me and her tears, I noticed, dried up instantly. She jumped up from her knees, muttered, "Oh Lord! . . ." and rushed out. The old woman vanished with her and the door was shut.

Ivan Vasilievich and I sat in silence. After a long pause he drummed his fingers on the table for a while.

"Well, how did you like that?" he asked and added wearily, "The curtain's ruined."

Another silence.

"I suppose that scene surprised you?" Ivan Vasilievich inquired and groaned.

I too groaned and fidgeted in my chair, at a complete loss what to reply: the scene had not, in fact, surprised me at all. I fully realized that it was a continuation of the scene which had taken place in the changing room and that Pryakhina had been carrying out her promise to throw herself at Ivan Vasilievich's feet.

"We were rehearsing," Ivan Vasilievich suddenly announced. "I suppose you thought that was simply a piece of scandal, didn't you?"

"Astounding," I said, concealing my expression.

"We like to refresh our memories with some little scene like that now and again . . . h'm, h'm . . . these études are very important . . . You mustn't believe what she said about Pelikan. Pelikan is a most useful and accomplished man!" Ivan Vasilievich gazed sadly at the curtain and said: "Well, let us continue!"

We could not continue because the same old woman had reappeared.

"My aunt, Nastasya Ivanovna," said Ivan Vasilievich.

I bowed. The charming old lady beamed at me, sat down and inquired, "And how are you?"

"Thank you very much," I replied with another bow, "I am quite well."

There was a further short silence while Ivan Vasilievich and his aunt looked at the curtain and exchanged a bitter glance.

"And what, pray, brings you to Ivan Vasilievich?"

"Leontii Sergeyevich," remarked Ivan Vasilievich, "has brought me a play."

"Whose play?" asked the old woman, gazing at me sorrowfully.

"Leontii Sergeyevich has written the play himself."

"What for?" asked Nastasya Ivanovna anxiously.

"What do you mean—what for? . . . H'm . . . h'm . . ."

"Aren't there enough plays already?" asked Nastasya Ivanovna in a tone of kindly reproach. "There are such lovely plays and so many of them! If you were to start playing them you couldn't get through them all in twenty years. Why do you want to write? It must be so upsetting!"

She was so convincing that I could find nothing to reply, but Ivan Vasilievich drummed his fingers and said, "Leontii Leontievich has written a *modern* play!"

This disturbed the old lady and she said: "We don't want to attack the government!"

"Why should anyone want to?" I said in her support.

"Don't you like *The Fruits of Enlightenment?*" asked Nastasya Ivanovna shyly and anxiously. "Such a nice play . . . and there's a part in it for dear Ludmilla . . ." She sighed and got up. "Please give my respects to your father."

"Sergei Sergeyevich's father is dead," put in Ivan Vasilievich.

"God rest his soul," said the old lady politely. "I don't suppose he knew you were writing a play, did he? What did he die of?"

"They called in the wrong doctor," said Ivan Vasilievich. "Leontii Paphnutievich has told me the whole distressing story."

"I didn't seem to catch your Christian name," said Nas-

120

tasya Ivanovna. "One moment it's Leontii, then it's Sergei! Do they allow people to change their Christian names too nowadays? One of our people changed his surname and now I never know who he is!"

"I am Sergei Leontievich," I said in a husky voice.

"A thousand pardons!" exclaimed Ivan Vasilievich. "My mistake!"

"Well, I won't disturb you," said the old lady.

"That cat should be whipped," said Ivan Vasilievich, "it's not a cat—it's a bandit. We suffer from bandits of all kinds," he added confidentially, "so badly that we don't know what to do!"

With the advancing twilight catastrophe struck.

I was reading:

" 'Bakhtin (To Petrov): Farewell. You will be following me soon . . .

"Petrov: What are you doing?

"Bakhtin shoots himself in the temple, falls. From afar comes the sound of an accordion . . .' "

"That won't do at all!" exclaimed Ivan Vasilievich. "Why did you write that? You must cross it out without a second's delay. Why, pray, must there be shooting?"

"But he has to die by committing suicide," I replied with a cough.

"Very well—let him die and let him stab himself with a dagger."

"But you see the action takes place during the Civil War . . . nobody used daggers by then . . ."

"No, they were used," objected Ivan Vasilievich, "I was told it by . . . what was his name . . . I've forgotten . . . what they used . . . You must cross out that shot!"

I was temporarily silenced by having made such an awful mistake and then read on, " '. . . accordion and isolated shots. A man carrying a rifle appears on the bridge. The moon . . .' "

"My God!" cried Ivan Vasilievich. "Shots! More shots! What a disaster! Look here, Leo . . . Look here, you must cut that scene, it's superfluous."

"I thought," I said, trying to speak as calmly as possible, "that this scene was the main one . . . In it, you see . . ."

"Quite wrong!" Ivan Vasilievich cut me off. "That scene is not only not the main one, it is unnecessary. Why? That character of yours—what's his name? . . ."

"Bakhtin."

"M'm, yes . . . yes, he stabs himself off stage," Ivan Vasilievich waved his hand toward the vague distance, "then another character enters and says to his mother 'Bakhteyev has stabbed himself!' "

"But there's no mother in the play," I said, gazing stupefied at the covered glass.

"Then there must be one! You must write her in. It's not difficult. It may seem difficult at first—there was no mother and suddenly there she is; but that's an illusion, it's very easy. There's the old woman sobbing at home and the man who brings her the news . . . You can call him Ivanov . . ."

"But Bakhtin's the hero! He has a soliloquy on the bridge . . . I thought . . ."

"Then Ivanov can speak his soliloquies. Your soliloquies are good, they must be kept. Ivanov can say: 'Petya has stabbed himself and before he died he said such and such . . .' It will make a very powerful scene."

"But how can I do that, Ivan Vasilievich? You see, there's a crowd scene on the bridge . . . The two sides clash . . ."

"Then you can make them clash off stage. We mustn't on any account see it. It's terrible when people clash on stage! You're lucky, Sergei Leonticvich," said Ivan Vasilievich, getting my name right for the first and only time, "that you don't know a man called Misha Panin!" (I turned cold.) "He is, I assure you, the most extraordinary person! We save him up for a rainy day, suddenly something happens and we let him loose! . . . He got us a new play recently and I may say that he did us no good with it—*Stenka Razin*. I arrived at the theater and as I was driving up I could hear from a considerable distance—the windows were open—crashing, whistling, shouts, curses and gunfire! The horse nearly bolted and I

thought there was a revolt in the theater. Horrible! It tran-
spired that Strizh was rehearsing! I said to Augusta Avdeyevna: 'What have you done? Do you want me to get shot?
Here's Strizh raking the theater with gunfire and nobody, I
suppose, has thought about the danger to me, have they?'
Augusta Avdeyevna, who is an admirable woman, replied:
'Punish me if you like, Ivan Vasilievich, I can't do a thing
with Strizh. That man Strizh is like a plague in this theater.'
If you ever see him I advise you to run a mile. (I turned cold
again.) Well, of course, all this had been done with the bless-
ing of someone called Aristarkh Platonovich. Luckily for you,
you don't know him, thank God . . . But *shots*—in your
play! Very well, let us continue."

So we continued and as darkness fell I said in a hoarse
voice, "The end."

Immediately I was seized by horror and despair. I had the
impression that I had built a little house and as soon as I had
moved into it the roof had collapsed.

"Very good," said Ivan Vasilievich when the reading was
over, "now you must start working on this material."

I wanted to scream "What?!"

But I didn't.

Now, Ivan Vasilievich, warming increasingly to his job,
began telling me exactly how I should rework my material.
The sister in the play should be changed into the mother. But
since the sister had a fiancé and as a fifty-year-old mother
(Ivan Vasilievich christened her Antonina) could not, of
course, have a fiancé, a character had to be eliminated and
what is more, a character I was very fond of.

Dusk crept into the room. The nurse appeared again and
once more Ivan Vasilievich took some drops. Then a wrin-
kled old woman brought in a table lamp and it was evening.

My head was in a whirl. Hammers were beating at my tem-
ples. I was so hungry that something seemed to be exploding
inside me and now and again the room swam before my
eyes. But worse of all the scene on the bridge had gone and
my hero with it. No, on second thoughts, the worst thing of

all was that some ghastly kind of misunderstanding had occurred. I suddenly saw in my mind's eye the poster announc-
ing my play; I could feel the last uneaten ten rubles of my
advance royalties crackling in my pocket; Thomas Strizh
seemed to be standing behind my back and assuring me that
the play would start running in two months' time: yet now it
was quite obvious that there was no play at all and that I
would have to start all over again and rewrite it from start to
finish. A wild witches' chorus of Misha Panin, Eulampia and
Strizh were dancing in front of me, I had visions of the scene
in the changing room, but of my play there was not a shred
left.

But then there occurred something completely unforseen
and even, to my mind, unimaginable . . .

Having demonstrated (and demonstrated very well) how
Bakhtin—whom Ivan Vasilievich had firmly renamed Bakhteyev should stab himself—he suddenly gave one of his
groans and announced:

"Now I'll tell you what sort of play you should write . . .
You could make a fortune with it overnight . . . A profound
psychological drama . . . The fate of an actress . . . Let's
say that in a certain country there lives an actress and a gang
of enemies is torturing her, persecuting her and giving her no
peace . . . And her only response is to pray for her enemies . . ."

"And make scenes," I thought to myself in a sudden access
of malice.

"Does she pray to God, Ivan Vasilievich?"

The question put Ivan Vasilicvich in a dilemma. He
groaned and answered:

"To God? H'm . . . h'm . . . No, on no account. You
mustn't put in anything about God . . . Not to God, but to
. . . art—art, to which she is profoundly dedicated. This
gang of villains persecutes her and they are egged on by a
wicked old wizard. You must describe how he has gone away
to Africa and transferred his magic powers to a certain Madame X. A terrible woman. She sits behind a desk and is utterly unscrupulous. If you sit down to tea with her, look care-

fully and you'll see that she puts a special sort of sugar into your cup . . ."

"Heavens above, he's talking about Toropetzkaya!" I thought.

". . . And when you drink it, it knocks you out. She and another frightful villain called Strizh . . . I mean, h'm . . . a certain producer . . ."

I sat there, staring vacantly at Ivan Vasilievich. The smile gradually slipped from his face and I suddenly saw that there was not a trace of kindness in his face.

"You, I can see, are a stubborn person," he said extremely gloomily and chewed his lips.

"No, Ivan Vasilievich, it's simply that the artistic world is so remote to me and . . ."

"Well, you must study it! It's very easy. There are personalities in our theater whom you cannot fail to admire. There's at least an act and a half's worth material ready-made for you! Then there are others who only wait for you to turn your back before they'll filch your shoes from the cloakroom or stick a Finnish knife in your ribs."

"How awful," I said as I tapped my forehead.

"I see that you don't find it amusing . . . You are a man of firm principles! Your play is a good one, too, by the way," announced Ivan Vasilievich looking searchingly at me, "all you have to do now is to write it . . . and everything will be ready . . ."

On tottering legs, with a pounding head I went out, staring resentfully at the black bust of Ostrovsky as I went. Muttering to myself, I stumped down the creaking wooden staircase; my play, which I had come to hate, hung in my hands like lead. As I walked out into the courtyard the wind blew off my hat and I had to pick it up out of a puddle. The Indian summer was gone without a trace. Rain was slanting down, water squelched underfoot, damp leaves were torn from the trees in the garden. A trickle ran down inside my collar. Muttering incoherent curses at life in general and at myself in particular

I walked on, glancing at the street lights glowing dimly through the cobweb of rain.

A feeble light was flickering in a street-corner kiosk. Newspapers held down by bricks lay on the counter getting wet and for no particular reason I bought a copy of *The Image of Melpomene* with a drawing on the cover of a man wearing a sweater, a quill in his cap and an exaggeratedly affected expression.

My room seemed to be more than usually loathsome. I threw my soaking typescript on to the floor, sat down at the table and pressed my hand to my temple to stop it hammering. With my other hand I fumbled for some crumbs of black bread and chewed them.

Removing my hand from my forehead I began to leaf through the damp copy of *The Image of Melpomene*. I noticed a picture of some woman in a crinoline, a headline which said "Pay attention," another which said "Tenor Di Grazia lets himself go" and then suddenly I caught a glimpse of my own surname. I was so amazed that my head even stopped aching. My name appeared again and again, then it was coupled with Lope de Vega. There was no doubt about it: I was reading an article entitled "Don't Foul Your Own Doorstep" and the hero of the article was myself. I forget exactly what it was about, but can vaguely remember how it began:

"It was dull on the slopes of Parnassus.

" 'Nothing ever happens here,' said Jean-Baptiste Molière with a yawn.

" 'Aye, 'tis tedious,' answered Shakespeare."

Further on, as far as I remember, a door opened and I entered—a black-haired young man with a thick script under my arm. It was quite clear that all the denizens of the Elysian Fields were laughing at me in the most malicious way. Shakespeare, Lope de Vega and the spiteful Molière who asked whether I hadn't written something rather like *Tartuffe* and Chekhov, whom I had always imagined from books as being the most tactful of men; but the most violent attack of all was

made by the author of the article who was called Volkodov.
It is amusing to recall it now, but my bitterness knew no
bounds. I paced up and down the room, feeling that I had
been baselessly slandered. Wild dreams of shooting Volkadov
alternated with puzzled reflection on what I might have done
to deserve this.

"The poster!" I whispered. "But I didn't print it, did I?
Take that!" I muttered as I saw a vision of a bloodstained
Volkodov falling at my feet.

Suddenly I smelled a whiff of pipe tobacco, the door
creaked and in came Likospastov wearing a wet mackintosh.

"Have you read it?" he asked delightedly. "Congratulations on your first critical review. You'll have to get used to
that sort of treatment in the writing game. As soon as I saw
it I came over here, as your friend, to tell you." And he hung
his dripping mackintosh on the hook.

"Who's this Volkodov?" I asked glumly.

"Why should you want to know?"

"Ah, so you know? . . ."

"But you've met him yourself."

"I don't know anyone called Volkodov!"

"Of course you do. I introduced you to him . . . Don't
you remember, in the street . . . that funny poster . . .
Sophocles and so on . . ."

Then I remembered the fat man who had stared thoughtfully at my hair . . . of course—"black hair"!

"What have I done to that son-of-a-bitch?" I burst out ve-
hemently.

Likospastov shook his head.

"Now, now, old boy, that's not the way . . . that won't do
at all. I can see that you've got a bad case of swollen head.
Can't anybody say a single word about you now? You won't
last long if you can't take criticism."

"What do you mean—'criticism'? That's not criticism!
it's libel! Who is this man?"

"He's a playwright," replied Likospastov. "He's written
five plays. And he's a splendid fellow, you're doing him an
injustice. Of course he's a bit put out . . . We all are . . ."

"But I didn't print that poster, did I? Is it my fault that Sophocles and Lope de Vega are in their repertoire and . . ."

"Well, you must admit that you're no Sophocles," said Likospastov with a malicious laugh. "Look at me—I've been writing for twenty-five years," he went on, "and even I haven't reached the Sophocles class yet . . ." He sighed.

I felt that I had nothing to say in reply to Likospastov. Nothing. How could I bring myself to say: "You haven't reached that class because you're a hopeless writer and I'm a good one"? I ask you how could I?

So I said nothing and Likospastov went on, "Of course, that poster did cause rather a stir. Lots of people have asked me about it. They think it's a bit offensive. Still, I didn't come here to argue. When I heard about your bit of bad luck I came over to cheer you up, have a talk . . ."

"What bit of bad luck?!"

"Ivan Vasilievich didn't like your play," said Likospastov, his eyes shining. "You read it to him today, didn't you?"

"How do you know?"

"Oh, the grapevine, you know . . ." said Likospastov with a sigh, obviously reveling in the situation.

"Do you know Nastasya Ivanovna Koldybayeva?" Without waiting for my reply he went on, "She's greatly esteemed—she's Ivan Vasilievich's aunt. All Moscow respects her and we've all begged favors of her in our time. She used to be a famous actress. There's a dressmaker living in our house called Anna Stupina. She had just come back from seeing Nastasya Ivanovna, who had told her all about it. Today, she said, some new man called on Ivan Vasilievich and read him his play. He looked as black as a black beetle (I immediately guessed that it was you). Ivan Vasilievich didn't like it, she said. Yes, she did! Now don't you remember what I told you when you first read it to us? I told you that the third act wasn't meaty enough, it was too superficial—don't be upset, I told you for your own good. And you wouldn't listen! After all, Ivan Vasilievich knows his job, you can't fool him—he spotted at once what was wrong with it. And if he doesn't

like it, you can take my word for it that the play won't be put
on. That poster's going to look a bit silly, now, isn't it? People
are going to laugh at you—there's a Euripides for you, they'll
say! Yes, and Nastasya Ivanovna said too that you'd annoyed
Ivan Vasilievich somehow, upset him? He started to give you
some advice and you just sniffed at him! Sniffed! I'm sorry,
old man, but really that's going a bit far! You can't behave
like that in your position! Ivan Vasilievich doesn't need your
play so badly that you can afford to sniff at him . . ."

"Let's go out to a restaurant," I said quietly, "I don't feel
like sitting at home . . ."

"I understand! Oh, how I understand!" exclaimed Likospastov. "I'd love to join you, but just now I'm a bit short
. . ." He fiddled uneasily with his wallet.

"I've got some money."

About half an hour later we were sitting behind a stained
tablecloth in the window of a little restaurant called the "Na-
ples." A pleasant man with fair hair served us, put some hors
d'oeuvres on the table, spoke nicely, called cucumbers
"cukes," recommended a "nice little bit of caviar" and gener-
ally made us feel so welcome that I managed to forget that the
street outside was in thick fog and I even stopped thinking
what a snake in the grass Likospastov was.

CHAPTER THIRTEEN

I PERCEIVE
THE TRUTH

THERE IS nothing worse, comrades, than faintness of heart and a lack of self-confidence. They brought me to the point where I began to wonder whether I ought not to change the sister-fiancée into the mother after all.

"Surely," I reasoned with myself, "he can't have been wrong. After all, it is his job to know about these things!" Picking up my pen I began writing. I frankly admit that the result was utter nonsense. The fact was that I had come to hate that unwanted mother Antonina so much that as soon as she appeared on paper I couldn't help grinding my teeth. Obviously it wouldn't work: you have to love your characters. If you don't I don't advise anybody to try writing; the result is bound to be unfortunate. Believe me, I know.

"I know!" I muttered hoarsely and, crumpling the sheet of

paper into tatters, I swore not to go back to the theater. It was agonizingly hard to keep my resolution. I still wanted to know how it would all work out. "No, let them beg me to come," I thought. One lonely day passed, then another, then three days, a week, and still no summons from the theater. "Obviously that swine Likospastov was right," I thought to myself, "they're not going to put my play on. So much for that poster, *Fenisa's Bait* and all! Oh, why don't they send for me?"

One day there was a knock on my door and in came Bombardov. I was so glad to see him that I was close to tears.

"All this was to be expected," said Bombardov, sitting on the window seat and swinging his foot against the radiator. "It happened just as I predicted. Don't say I didn't warn you!"

"But put yourself in my place, Pyotr Petrovich," I cried. "How could I avoid reading the passage about the shot? How could I?"

"Well, you read it and look what happened," said Bombardov cruelly.

"I shall never part with my hero," I said angrily.

"But there's no question of parting with him . . ."

"Oh yes there is!" Gasping with indignation I told Bombardov about everything—about the mother, about Petya who was supposed to take over my hero's favorite soliloquies and about the dagger, which particularly infuriated me.

"How would you like to be told to do all that?" I asked challengingly.

"It's rubbish," replied Bombardov, instinctively glancing around.

"Well then!"

"But you shouldn't have argued," said Bombardov softly. "You should have said 'Thank you very much, Ivan Vasilievich, for your suggestions and I shall certainly do my best to carry them out.' It's no good answering back, don't you see? At Sivtsev Vrazhek nobody ever answers back."

"You can't mean it?! Nobody—ever?"

"Nobody," replied Bombardov, emphasizing every word,

"has answered back, does answer back or ever will answer back."

"Whatever he may say?"

"Whatever he may say."

"And supposing he were to say that my main character ought to go to Penza? Or that this mother, Antonina, ought to hang herself? Or that she sings contralto? Or that that stove is black? What do I have to say to that?"

"That the stove *is* black."

"What will the stove be like in the actual stage set?"

"White with a black spot."

"This is monstrous, unheard of . . ."

"No, it isn't. We manage," replied Bombardov.

"But look here—won't Aristarkh Platonovich have something to say to him?"

"Aristarkh Platonovich won't have anything to say to him because Aristarkh Platonovich hasn't been on speaking terms with Ivan Vasilievich since 1885."

"You're not serious?"

"They quarreled in 1885 and since then they haven't met and they haven't even spoken to each other on the telephone."

"You're making my head spin. How does the theater keep going?"

"It keeps going, as you can see, and very well too. They have each marked off their areas of responsibility. If, for instance, it had been Ivan Vasilievich who had first taken an interest in your play, Aristarkh Platonovich wouldn't have had anything to do with it and vice versa. Like that they avoid any grounds for a clash. It's a very wise system."

"Oh Lord—and now, of all times, Aristarkh Platonovich has to be in India. If he were here I would have gone to him and . . ."

"H'm . . ." said Bombardov, looking out of the window.

"How can one deal with a man who never listens to anybody?"

"No, he does listen sometimes. He listens to three people —Gavriil Stepanovich, his aunt Nastasya Ivanovna and Augusta Avdeyevna. Those are the three people on earth who can influence Ivan Vasilievich. If anybody except them imagines he can influence Ivan Vasilievich, all he succeeds in doing is to make Ivan Vasilievich do the opposite."

"Why?"

"He doesn't trust anybody . . ."

"But that's terrible!"

"Every great man has his foibles," said Bombardov, trying to mollify me.

"Very well. I think I understand the situation. It seems hopeless. If the only way of having my play staged is to distort it until it becomes meaningless, then there's no point in staging it at all. I don't want the audiences thinking that I'm mentally deficient because it sees a man in the twentieth century, armed with a revolver, stab himself with a dagger."

"They won't think that because there won't be any dagger. Your hero will shoot himself like any normal person."

I quieted down.

"If you would only behave calmly," Bombardov went on, "and listen to advice, you would have agreed to the dagger and to Antonina and in the end neither of them would have appeared in the play. There are ways and means of doing everything."

"What ways and means?"

"Misha Panin knows what they are," replied Bombardov in a sepulchral voice.

"And now, I suppose, everything is ruined?" I inquired miserably.

"Well, it's tricky, very tricky," was Bombardov's depressing reply.

Two weeks had passed and there was still no news from the theater. My wounded feelings had gradually healed and the only unbearable thought was the possibility of going back to the *Shipping Gazette* and having to write articles again.

But suddenly . . . Oh, that accursed word! . . . As I leave this world forever, I bear with me a cowardly, invincible fear of that word. I fear it as much as I fear words like "Guess what?" "You're wanted on the telephone," "There's a telegram for you" or "Will you please come to the office." I know only too well what follows words like these. Suddenly, as I said, and completely unexpected, I received a visit from Demyan Kosmich, who shuffled his feet and handed me a note asking me to come to the theater on the following day at four o'clock in the afternoon.

There was no rain next day; it was a day of sharp autumn frost. My heels ringing on the asphalt, worried, I made my way to the theater. There the first thing that met my eyes was a cab horse, so overfed that it looked more like a rhinoceros, and a desiccated old man seated on the driver's box. Instinctively I realized in a flash that it was Drykin. This worried me even more. Inside the theater I was surprised by a certain feeling of excitement everywhere. There was no one in Phil's office and his petitioners or rather the most persistent of them were crowded into the courtyard, freezing with cold and occasionally peering in at the window. Some even tried tapping on the panes, but without any result. I knocked at the door which opened a little way to reveal Bakvalin's eyes in the gap and I heard Phil's voice saying, "Let him in at once!"

I was admitted. Some of the unfortunates in the courtyard made an attempt to push in behind me, but the door closed on them. Tripping over the steps with a crash, I was picked up by Bakvalin and went into the office. Phil was not in his usual place but in the front room. He was wearing a new tie —a spotted one, I remember—and had shaved with unusual care.

He greeted me with a particular solemnity tinged with a hint of sorrow. Something important was going on in the theater (I sensed it in the way that an ox must sense it is being led away to be pole-axed) in which I, for once, was cast in the leading role. This was even detectable in the short phrase which Phil addressed in a low but peremptory tone to Bakvalin, "Take his overcoat!"

All the messengers and commissionaires were behaving oddly. Not one of them was sitting down at his post, but were all in a state of uneasy activity baffling to the uninitiated.

Demyan Kozmich for instance came up at a fast trot, over-
took me and passed on silently upstairs to the dress circle. No
sooner had he disappeared than down came Kuskov, also at a
trot, likewise to vanish again. In the darkened lobby Klyukvin
was loitering nervously and for no apparent reason he drew
the curtain on one of the windows, then disappeared without
trace leaving the other curtains open. Bakvalin padded past
me on the soundless broadcloth and vanished into the buffet,
whence emerged Panin to scuttle into the auditorium.

"Upstairs with me, please," said Phil as he politely showed
me the way.

Up we went. Someone else shot past me without a sound
and made for the upper circle. I began to feel that the shades
of the dead were flitting around me. When we had made our
silent way to the doors of the changing room I saw Demyan
Kozmich standing on guard. Some figure in a jacket made a
dash for the door, but Demyan Kozmich gave a strangled
screech, spreadeagled himself across the doorway and the figure swerved and disappeared into the gloom of a staircase.

"Let him in!" whispered Phil and vanished.

Demyan Kozmich leaned on the door, I was let through
and . . . through another door . . . then I was in the
brightly lit changing room. A light was burning on Toropetzkaya's desk. She was not typing but sitting and reading a
newspaper. She nodded to me.

At the door leading into the director's office stood Menazhraki in a green jumper with a diamond cross round her
neck and a large bunch of shiny keys hanging from her patent-
leather belt.

She said: "This way"—and I found myself in a brilliantly lit
room. The first thing that I noticed was the expensive furniture of Karelian birch with gold inlay, a gigantic desk of the
same material and a black bust of Ostrovsky in the corner. A
chandelier shone beneath the ceiling, sconces on the walls. I
had a sudden impression that the portraits from the gallery
had stepped down from their frames and were moving toward me. I recognized Ivan Vasilievich, who was sitting on a
couch in front of a round occasional table on which stood a

glass jar of jam. I also recognized Knyazhevich and several other people from their portraits, including an unusually imposing lady in a scarlet blouse, a brown jacket sprinkled with buttons like stars and topped by a sable fur. A little hat was perched jauntily on her graying hair, her eyes shone under black brows and her fingers glittered with several heavy diamond rings.

There were some people in the room who did not figure in the portrait gallery. Behind the couch was the same doctor who had made such a timely appearance to save Ludmilla Pryakhina from fainting and who was still holding a tumbler, while the buffet-attendant stood in the doorway wearing his usual woebegone look. The large table by the wall was covered with a dazzlingly white tablecloth. Lights flashed on crystal and porcelain, lights were dully reflected from seltzer bottles and there was a glimpse of what I think was red caviar. The large gathering, reclining in armchairs, made a vague movement as I entered and returned my bow.

"Ah! Leo . . ." Ivan Vasilievich started to say.

"Sergei Leontievich," Knyazhevich hastily put in.

"Yes . . . Welcome, Sergei Leontievich! Do sit down, I beg of you!" Ivan Vasilievich shook me firmly by the hand. "Wouldn't you like a bite of something? Perhaps you'd care for a spot of lunch? Do say if you would. We're in no hurry. Our Yermolai Ivanovich is a wizard, you only have to tell him what you want and—Yermolai Ivanovich, have we something to give our friend for lunch?"

In reply the wizard Yermolai Ivanovich rolled his eyes upward, then rolled them down again and beamed me an imploring look.

"Or perhaps a drink?" Ivan Vasilievich continued to press me. "Seltzer? Lemonade? Cranberry? Yermolai Ivanovich!" said Ivan Vasilievich sternly, "have we got enough cranberry? Make sure that we have, please!" Yermolai Ivanovich smiled shyly and hung his head. "As I said, Yermolai Ivanovich is a . . . h'm, h'm . . . magician. When things were at their most desperate he saved every one of us from starvation by feeding us with sturgeon! Otherwise we could have all per-ished to a man. The actors worship him!" Far from appearing proud of the feat, Yermolai Ivanovich's face clouded over more profoundly than ever.

In a clear, firm, resonant voice I announced that I had already lunched and I categorically declined the offer of seltzer and lemonade.

"Then some cake perhaps? Yermolai Ivanovich is famous all over the world for his pastries!"

In a voice of even greater firmness and power (afterward Bombardov told me how the other people present had described me and he said: "What a voice you put on!" "What was wrong with it?" "Thin, hoarse, disagreeable . . .") I also declined the cake.

"Talking of cake," suddenly came the deep, velvet bass voice of an exquisitely dressed and barbered man with fair hair, who was sitting beside Ivan Vasilicvich, "I remember once we were all at Pruchevin's, and who should come in but the grand duke Maximilian Petrovich. How we laughed . . . You know Pruchevin, don't you, Ivan Vasilievich? Some other time I'll tell you the funny story of what happened."

"I know Pruchevin," replied Ivan Vasilievich. "The biggest rogue alive. He once stripped his own sister bare in . . . Aha!"

At this point the door admitted another person besides myself who did not figure in the portrait gallery—Misha Panin. "Yes, he shot his friend . . ." I thought as I looked at his face.

"Ah, our invaluable Mikhail Alexeyevich!" cried Ivan Vasilievich, stretching out his arms toward him. "Do come in! Take a seat. Let me introduce you," Ivan Vasilievich turned to me, "This is our precious Mikhail Alexeyevich who does such great work for us. And this is is . . ."

"Sergei Leontievich!" put in Knyazhevich gaily.

"Exactly!"

Without admitting that we knew each other already yet without denying it either, Misha and I simply shook hands.

"Now let's get down to business!" announced Ivan Vasilievich. I squirmed as all eyes turned on me. "Who has something to say? Hippolyte Pavlovich!" A man of striking appearance, dressed with great taste, his head crowned with curls the shade of a raven's wing, screwed his monocle into his eye and fixed its glare on me. Then he poured himself a glass of seltzer, drank it, wiped his mouth with a silk handkerchief, hesitated—should he drink another glass or not?—drank a second glassful and began to speak. He had a wonderfully soft, consciously modulated voice, penetrating and instantly convincing.

"Your novel, Le . . . Sergei Leontievich, isn't it? Your novel is very, very good . . . It is . . . er . . . how shall I put it? . . ." Here the orator leaned toward the big table, loaded with seltzer bottles, and Yermolai Ivanovich at once minced toward him and handed him a fresh bottle, "charged with psychological profundity, the characters are drawn with extraordinary truth . . . er . . . As for the descriptions of nature, there I would say you have touched heights which are almost worthy of Turgenev!" Seltzer bubbled into the glass, the orator drank a third glassful and dropped the monocle from his eye with a simple movement of his eyebrow. "Those descriptions," he went on, "of the southern countryside . . . er . . . the starry Ukrainian nights . . . then the rustle of the Dnieper . . . er . . . how did Gogol describe it . . . er . . . the 'Glorious Dnieper,' you remember the passage . . . and the scent of acacia . . . it is all masterly, quite masterly . . ."

I glanced at Misha Panin. He was hunched defensively in his chair, but his eyes were terrible.

"I found especially vivid that . . . er . . . description of a wood . . . the silvery poplar leaves . . . do you remember?"

"In my mind's eye I can still remember those nights on the Dnieper when we went there on tour," said a contralto lady in sables.

"Talking of that tour," echoed the bass beside Ivan Vasilievich and laughed, "there was a deliciously piquant situation with Dukabasov, the governor-general. Do you remember him, Ivan Vasilievich?"

"I do. A most fearful glutton," said Ivan Vasilievich. "But go on."

"I have nothing but praise for . . . er, er . . . your novel . . . but . . . forgive my frankness—the stage has its own laws."

Ivan Vasilievich sat eating jam as he listened with pleasure to Hippolyte Pavlovich.

"In the play you have not quite succeeded in putting across the whole atmosphere of the south, of those warm southern nights. The characters seemed to me psychologically inadequate, especially the part of Bakhtin . . ." Here the speaker seemed unaccountably to lose his temper and began spluttering, "P . . . p . . . and I . . . er, er . . . I don't know how . . ." He banged the rim of his monocle against a rolled-up typescript, which I recognized as my play. "The part's unplayable . . . I'm sorry," he finished, by now thoroughly offended, "I'm sorry!" Our glances met and in mine he saw, I trust, fury, malice and amazement. The fact is that in my novel there was not a word about acacias, silvery poplars, the rustling Dnieper or any of the things he had described.

"He hasn't read it! He hasn't read my novel," the words rang in my head, "yet he has the cheek to talk about it . . . that stuff about the Ukrainian nights—he's made it all up! What on earth have they asked me here for?"

"Has anyone else got anything to say?" said Ivan Vasilievich with a cheerful glance around the room. There was a tense silence. Nobody wanted to speak. Then came a voice from the corner, "Ah h'm, h'm . . ." I turned my head and saw in the corner a stout elderly man in a dark blouse. I vaguely remembered his face on one of the portraits . . . His eyes were kind, his general look expressed profound boredom and disillusion. As I looked at him he averted his eyes.

"Were you going to say something, Fyodor Vladimirovich?" said Ivan Vasilievich.

"No," was the reply.

There was something odd about the silence. Ivan Vasilievich turned to me and inquired, "Would you like to say something?"

In a voice that was by now unresonant, unclear and utterly uncheerful—even I realized that—I said, "As I see it, my play is unsuitable. Kindly hand it back to me."

My little speech caused consternation. Chairs moved uneasily, someone leaned over me from behind my back and said: "No, you can't say that! Really!"

Ivan Vasilievich stared at the jam, then gazed in astonishment at the people around him.

"H'm . . . h'm . . ." He started drumming his fingers. "We are trying to tell you in the most friendly way that to produce your play would cause you the most fearful harm! Terrible harm! Especially if Thomas Strizh produces it. You'd regret it all your life and you would curse us . . ."

After a pause I said: "In that case please give it back to me."

It was then that I clearly detected the glitter of malice in Ivan Vasilievich's eyes.

"There is the little matter of a contract," suddenly a voice rang out and from behind the doctor's back appeared the face of Gavriil Stepanovich.

"But if your theater doesn't want to produce it, what good is it to you?"

A face with very lively eyes behind a pince-nez moved in my direction and said in a high tenor: "You wouldn't take it to the Shlippe Theater, would you? Look what they do to plays there. They'd have the characters strutting about like Prussian officers. Who wants to see that sort of thing?"

"As the law and its interpretation stands at present you can't give the play to the Shlippe, we have a contract!" said Gavriil Stepanovich stepping out from behind the doctor.

"What's happening here? What do they want?" I thought and for the first time in my life I sensed a terrible feeling of asphyxia. "I'm sorry," I said dully, "but I still don't understand. You don't want to produce the play yet I can't offer it to another theater. It doesn't make sense."

These words produced an extraordinary effect. The lady in

the sables exchanged an outraged look with the bass on the couch. But most terrible of all was the look on Ivan Vasilievich's face. The smile vanished and I received the full stare of his angry, burning eyes.

"We want to save you from fearful harm," said Ivan Vasilievich, "from certain danger which is lurking to pounce on you."

Silence returned and it grew so agonizing that I could bear it no longer. After scratching the upholstery of the armchair for a few moments I got up and bowed myself out. They all returned my bow except Ivan Vasilievich, who was staring at me in amazement. I backed my way to the door, tripped, went out, bowed to Toropetzkaya who was looking at *Izvestiya* with one eye and watching me with the other, bowed to Augusta Menazhraki, who took it coldly, and left.

The theater was deep in twilight. White blobs could be seen in the buffet—the tables had been laid for the evening show. A door into the auditorium was open, so I stopped for a few moments and gazed in. The stage was open on all sides, as far as the brick wall. A green, plush-furnished summerhouse was being lowered from above, from the sides antlike workmen were maneuvering some white pillars onto the stage through the huge open doors.

A minute later I had left the theater.

As Bombardov had no telephone I sent him that evening a telegram which read: "You are invited to a wake in memory deceased. Shall go mad without you please explain." The post office at first refused to accept this telegram until I threatened to complain to the *Shipping Gazette*.

Next evening Bombardov and I were sitting at table together. My neighbor's wife had brought me some blini. Bombardov liked my idea of holding a wake and he liked my room, which I had made quite tidy and comfortable.

"I've got over my disappointment by now," I said after my guest had taken the edge off his appetite, "but I just want to know one thing: how could it happen? I am simply tortured with curiosity. I have never seen such an extraordinary business in my life."

Bombardov replied by praising the blini, looking around the room and saying, "You should get married, Sergei Leontievich. Marry some charming, tender woman or girl."

"Gogol wrote that line," I countered, "so let's not bother to repeat it. Tell me how it happened."

Bombardov shrugged his shoulders.

"There was nothing special. Ivan Vasilievich held a meeting of the senior members of the theater, that's all."

"I know that. Who was that woman in sables?"

"Margarita Petrovna Tavricheskaya, an actress who is one of the theater's senior or founder members. She's famous because in 1885 Ostrovsky said 'Very good' when she made her debut."

I further discovered that the people in the room had consisted exclusively of founder members who had been summoned to an extraordinary session on account of my play, that Drykin had been notified the day before and had spent hours grooming his horse and cleaning the cab with carbolic. I found out that the man who had told the stories about the grand duke Maximilian Petrovich and the gluttonous governor-general was the youngest of the founder members.

I should add that Bombardov's replies were marked by obvious restraint and discretion. Noticing this, I tried to twist my questions so as to make him give me more than just dry, formal answers such as "he was born in such-and-such a year, his name is so-and-so" and instead to describe something of their characters. I was profoundly interested in those people who had foregathered in the director's office. I assumed that a knowledge of their characters would enable me to piece together an explanation of their behavior at that curious meeting.

"So this Gornostayev (the man who told the governor-general story) is a good actor, is he?" I asked, pouring out some wine for Bombardov.

"Uh-huh," replied Bombardov.

"Come on, now—what does 'uh-huh' mean? Now, for instance, I know that Margarita Petrovna is famous because Ostrovsky said Very good.' Fine—anyone would be proud to have scored that. You can't just put me off with 'uh-huh.' Isn't Gornostayev famous for something too?"

Bombardov gave me a careful, surreptitious look and muttered, "What can I tell you about him? H'm . . ." and emptying his glass he said, "Well, Gornostayev did, in fact, amaze everybody a short while ago with something extraordinary that happened to him . . ." Here he began pouring melted butter on his blini and poured for so long that I exclaimed, "For God's sake, don't keep me on tenterhooks!"

"Delicious, this Georgian wine," said Bombardov, trying my patience to the utmost, then he went on, "It happened four years ago, in early spring as far as I remember, and at a time when Gornostayev was in very good form and particularly cheerful. He was hatching some plans to go away somewhere and was so excited that he even seemed to get younger. I should tell you that he is passionately fond of the theater. I remember how he used to say at the time, 'Ah, I'm getting out of date. There was a time when I kept up with theatrical life in the West. I used to go abroad every year and of course I knew everything that was going on in the theater in Germany and France. And even further afield than France—I went to America once for a look at the latest developments in the theater there.' 'Well,' people said to him, 'why don't you apply for permission and go now?' He would give a sort of gentle smile and reply, 'I wouldn't dream of it. This is not the time for people like me to go jaunting abroad. Do you think I'd let the state spend its precious foreign currency on me? Much better let some engineer or economist go.' Noble sentiments! Well now . . ." Bombardov squinted through his glass at the lamplight and praised the wine again. "Well now, a month went by and spring was really upon us. Then came disaster. One day Gornostayev came into Augusta Avdeyevna's office. He didn't say a word. She looked at him, saw that his face looked as white as a sheet and was set in a funeral expression. 'What's the matter?' 'Nothing,' he replied, 'don't bother about me.' He went over to the window, drummed his fingers on the glass and begin to whistle a sad, terribly familiar snatch of music. She listened for a moment and recognized Chopin's *Funeral March*. Unable to contain herself, filled with human kindness, she asked, 'What's the matter? What is it?' He turned toward her, gave a lopsided smile and said: 'Swear that you won't tell anybody!' She, of course, immediately gave her solemn oath. 'I've just been to see the doctor and he has found that I've got a slight cancer of the lung.' With that he turned and went out."

"How awful," I said quietly, feeling quite ill.

"Wasn't it!" said Bombardov. "Well, Augusta Avdeyevna at once swore Gavriil Stepanovich to secrecy and told him, he told Hippolyte Pavlovich, he told his wife, his wife told Eulampia Petrovna. To cut a long story short, in two hours' time even the assistants in the costume-maker's workshop knew that Gornostayev's acting career was at an end and they might as well start ordering a wreath. Within three hours the actors in the buffet were already discussing who was to get Gornostayev's parts.

"Meanwhile Augusta Avdeyevna picked up the telephone and rang Ivan Vasilievich. Exactly three days later Augusta Avdeyevna rang up Gornostayev's apartment and said: 'I'm coming to see you right away.' And come she did. Gornostayev was lying on a sofa wearing a Chinese dressing gown, pale as death itself, but calm and proud.

"Augusta Avdeyevna is an efficient woman and she threw down on the table a passport and a checkbook—bang! Gornostayev flinched and said, 'You wicked people. I didn't want that. Why should I have to die abroad?' Augusta Avdeyevna, brave, loyal secretary that she is, paid no attention and shouted, 'Ivan!' Ivan is Gornostayev's devoted servant and he appeared immediately.

" 'The train leaves in three hours. Get his traveling rug! Underclothes! Suitcase! Dressing case! The car will be here in forty minutes.' The doomed man only sighed and waved his hand.

"There's a place, not exactly on the Swiss side of the frontier, not quite outside Switzerland, somewhere in the

144

Alps . . ." Bombardov wiped his forehead, "anyway it
doesn't matter where it is precisely. At a height of ten thousand feet above sea level there is a world-famous high-altitude
sanatorium run by a Professor Klee. They only send desperate
cases there—it's all or nothing. They don't get any worse and
sometimes miracles do happen. Klee puts these hopeless creatures on an open veranda in sight of the snow-covered peaks,
gives them injections, makes them breathe oxygen and Klee
has cured some of them inside a year.

"A quarter of an hour later, Gornostayev was driven, at his
own wish, past the theater . . . Demyan Kozmich told me
afterward that he saw Gornostayev raise his hand and bless
the theater, then the car turned the corner and drove him off
to the Belorussky Station.

"Summer came and with it a rumor that Gornostayev had
died. Everybody gossiped about it, sympathized with his fam-
ily . . . But it was summer and the actors were getting ready
to leave Moscow, some of them were already on holiday . . .
Somehow they weren't quite as grief-stricken as they might
have been . . . They waited for Gornostayev's body to be
brought back. Meanwhile the actors left town, the season
came to an end. However, our good Plisov . . ."

"That's the nice-looking man with moustaches, isn't it?" I
asked. "That one in the portrait gallery?"

"That's the one," Bombardov confirmed and went on,
"Well, he was sent away to Paris to study stage machinery. He
got his travel documents at once and left. Plisov, I should
mention, is an incredibly hard worker and is literally in love
with his revolving stage. We all envied him. Who wouldn't
like a free trip to Paris? 'Lucky fellow,' we all said. Lucky or
not, he took his passport and set off for Paris at the very time
when the rumor was going around that Gornostayev had
died. Plisov is a bit of an eccentric and he made a point while
he was in Paris of not even seeing the Eiffel Tower. He's mad
about his work. He spent the whole time sitting in the dark
under stages, bought himself a flashlight, studied everything he
had to and made a thorough job of it. At last the time came
for him to leave. He decided to take a walk around Paris and

at least to have a look at it before returning home. He walked and walked, took bus rides, chiefly making himself understood by shouting and finished up so hungry that he was ready to go anywhere for a meal. 'I'll go to some little restaurant,' he thought, 'and have a bite to eat.' He saw a brightly lit restaurant and because it was away from the center he felt it ought not to be too expensive. So in he went and it was, in fact, a pretty mediocre sort of restaurant. As he walked in and looked around he stood frozen to the spot.

"There, sitting at a table and wearing a dinner jacket, a flower in his buttonhole, was the late lamented Gornostayev and with him a couple of French girls who at that very moment were in fits of laughter. In front of them was a bottle of champagne in an ice bucket and a dish of fruit salad.

"Plisov had to clutch the doorway to stop himself falling over. 'It can't be,' he thought. 'I must be seeing things. That can't be Gornostayev sitting there and laughing. There's only one place he can be—in Novodevichy Cemetery!'

"He stood there goggling at this creature, so horribly like the dead man, who got up with a distinctly worried look. Plisov even had the impression that the man was displeased at seeing him, but Gornostayev told him later that he had merely been surprised. Gornostayev, for it was he, whispered something to the two French girls who immediately vanished.

"Plisov only came to his senses when Gornostayev embraced him. He explained everything. All that Plisov could say was 'Well I never!'

"Gornostayev had been brought to the Alps in such a condition that Klee could only shake his head and say 'H'm . . .' Well, they put Gosnostayev on the veranda, injected him with the famous serum and put him in an oxygen tent. At first the patient got worse, so much worse in fact that Klee, as Gornostayev admitted later, did not expect him to survive another twenty-four hours because his heart was so weak. However, the next day there was an improvement. The injections were repeated. The day after that he was better still and from then onward his progress was quite incredible. Gornostayev sat up on his couch and said 'I think I'll take a walk now.' Even Klee himself was dumbfounded. After another day Gornostayev was walking round the veranda, his face was pink again and his appetite had come back. Temperature 98.4, pulse normal, not a trace of illness.

"According to Gornostayev people came from the surrounding villages to look at him. Doctors arrived from all over the country, Klee gave a lecture and declared that a case like this only occurred once in a thousand years. They wanted to put Gornostayev's picture in the medical journals but he flatly refused: 'I don't like publicity.'

"Klee then told Gornostayev that there was nothing more he could do for him in the Alps and that he was sending him to Paris to recuperate from his shattering experience. So that was why Gornostayev was in Paris. As for the two French girls, he explained, they were two newly qualified lady doctors who were gathering material to write an article about him. Some story!"

"Yes, it's amazing," I remarked, "but I still don't understand how he managed to get away so quickly?"

"That's the amazing thing," replied Bombardov. "Apparently as a result of the first injection Gornostayev's cancerous sarcoma started to shrivel and disappear."

I threw up my hands.

"You can't mean it!" I exclaimed. "But that never happens!"

"It happens once in a thousand years," said Bombardov and went on: "But wait, that's not all. That autumn Gornostayev came back to Moscow wearing a new suit, quite recovered and with a beautiful suntan—after Paris his French doctors had sent him on a cruise. In the theater buffet the other actors clustered around him listening to his stories about his ocean cruise, Paris, Swiss doctors and so on. Well, the season went on as usual; Gornostayev acted, indeed acted very well and everything was fine until March. Then in March Gornostayev suddenly appeared at a rehearsal of *The Lady Macbeth of Mtsensk* with some kind of virus infection. 'What's the matter?' 'Nothing, just a funny stabbing feeling in the small of my back.' Well, the stabbing pain went on. We expected it to stop, but it didn't. It went on and it got worse . . . He tried ultraviolet-ray treatment, but it was no good . . . Insomnia, couldn't sleep on his back. He grew visibly thinner. He tried 'Pantopon.' No good. Nothing for it but to see the doctor. And what do you think? . . ."

Bombardov made a well-timed pause and gave me a look that sent a shiver down my spine.

"And what do you think . . . the doctor examined him, pummeled him, blinked . . . Gornostayev said to him, 'Doctor, don't spare me, I'm not an old woman, I've been through plenty in my time . . . tell me—is it?' It was!" screamed Bombardov hoarsely and drained his glass at a gulp. "The cancer had come back again! It had moved to his right kidney and was devouring Gornostayev! Naturally it caused a sensation. No more rehearsals, Gornostayev was packed off home. This time, though, it was easier. Now there was hope. Again he had a passport in three days and a ticket to the Alps to see Klee. He greeted Gornostayev like a son, as well he might, since his cure had made him world famous! Out onto the veranda again, more injections—and the same story! In twenty-four hours the pain had gone, in two days Gornostayev was strolling about the veranda and in three days he was asking Klee whether he couldn't play a game of tennis. The effect on the sanatorium was incredible. Patients came flocking to Klee in droves! According to Gornostayev they started building a second hospital block alongside the original one. Klee, normally an extremely reserved man, kissed Gornostayev three times in the Russian fashion and sent him, as was only proper, to recuperate, only this time to Nice, then to Paris and then to Sicily.

"Once again Gornostayev came home in the autumn—we had just returned from a touring season in the Donbass coal-mining country—fresh, jaunty and healthy. Only his suit was different; the previous autumn it had been chocolate-colored, now it was gray with a light check. For three days he told us all about Sicily and how the bourgeois played roulette in Monte Carlo. It was a disgusting sight, he said. Again came the season and again spring the same complaint, only in a different place. A relapse, this time below his left knee. Off to Klee again, then to Madeira and a trip to Paris to round it off.

"By now, of course, there was no longer much anxiety over his recurrent cancer. Everybody realized that Klee had found the answer. Every year, apparently, the virulence of the cancer would be reduced under the influence of Klee's injections and the professor hoped, indeed he was convinced, that after another three or four seasons Gornostayev's physique would be able to counter unaided any reappearance of the cancer. Actually it recurred the year before last as no more than a mild pain in his sinus and went again as soon as Klee treated it. But now Gornostayev is under the strictest observation and whether he has any pain or not, he is automatically sent abroad every April."

"Incredible!" I said with a sigh.

Meanwhile our little celebration was well under way, our heads were getting fuddled with the Georgian wine, the talk grew livelier and above all franker. "You're a very interesting, observant and malicious man," I thought to myself about Bombardov, "and I like you very much, but you are cunning and secretive and it's living in the theater that has made you like that . . ."

"Don't be secretive!" I suddenly begged my guest. "Tell me, because I'll admit that I feel miserable—is my play really as bad as all that?"

"Your play," said Bombardov, "is a good play. Full stop."

"Then why, why, was I made to go through that terrible, agonizing scene in the director's office? Didn't they like my play?"

"No," said Bombardov firmly. "On the contrary. It all happened just *because* they liked it. And liked it very much indeed."

"But Hippolyte Pavlovich . . ."

"It was Hippolyte Pavlovich who liked it most of us," said Bombardov weightily and carefully and I thought I caught a look of sympathy in his eyes.

"It's enough to drive one mad . . ." I muttered.

"No, you mustn't give way. It's simply that you don't know what the theater's like. There are some complicated mechanisms in this world but the theater is the most complicated of them all . . ."

"Tell me about it! Tell me!" I cried, clutching my head.

"They liked your play so much that it put them into a panic," Bombardov began, "hence all the upheaval. As soon as they had read it and the old stagers heard about it they immediately started casting it. Hippolyte Pavlovich was to play Bakhtin, Petrov was to be given to Valentine Konradovich."

"What! Was he the one who . . . ?"

"Yes, that was him."

"But look here!" I said, more in a roar than a shout, "they're . . ."

"I know, I know," interrupted Bombardov, who obviously understood what was troubling me before I even had time to say it, "Hippolyte Pavlovich is sixty-one, Valentine Konradovich is sixty-two . . . How old is the oldest of your characters, Bakhtin, supposed to be?"

"Twenty-eight!"

"I thought so. Well, as soon as the senior actors were handed their scripts, the uproar was indescribable. There hasn't been anything like it in all the theater's fifty years of existence. They were all simply furious."

"With whom? With the casting director?"

"No. With the author."

The only thing left for me was to stare at him with bulging eyes. Bombardov went on:

"With the author. The old stagers, you see, reacted like this: we are actors, we want decent parts, we the founder members are longing for a good modern play in which we can show off our paces and . . . what happens? A man in a gray suit comes and brings a play in which the characters are scarcely even grown up! So we can't play it! Did he bring it here for a joke, or what? The very youngest of the founder members—Gornostayev—is fifty-five!"

"But I don't think my play's good enough to be acted by

the founder members!" I roared. "Give the parts to the young actors!"

"Oh, very clever!" cried Bombardov pulling a diabolical face. "Of course—let Argunin, Galin, Yelagin, Blagosvetlov and Strenkovsky act it and get all the applause! Bravo! Encore! Hurrah! Look at us, good people, see how well we act! And the founder members, I suppose, can sit around and watch and look embarrassed—and tell each other they're not wanted any more and that it's time for them to retire to the workhouse? Ha, ha, ha! Oh, clever—very clever!"

"I see!" I shouted in an effort to imitate his Satanic voice, "I see it all!"

"It's obvious," interrupted Bombardov. "Look—Ivan Vasilievich told you, didn't he, that you had to turn the fiancée into the mother so that Margarita Petrovna or Nastasya Ivanovna could have played her . . ."

"Nastasya Ivanovna?!"

"You're not a man of the theater," said Bombardov with a patronizing smile.

"Just tell me one thing," I said impulsively, "who was to have played Anna?"

"Ludmilla Pryakhina, of course."

This infuriated me.

"What? What!? Ludmilla Silvestrovna?!" I jumped out of my seat. "You must be joking!"

"Why, what's the matter?" asked Bombardov with amused curiosity.

"How old is she?"

"That, I'm afraid, is a mystery to us all."

"Anna is nineteen! Nineteen! Don't you see? But that's not the point! The point is that she can't act!"

"You mean she couldn't play Anna?"

"Not just Anna—she can't act at all!"

"I beg your pardon!"

"No, I mean it! An actress trying to play the part of someone being persecuted and humiliated, and who plays it so badly that she frightens the cat into tearing the curtain into shreds, can't act at all."

"That cat is an idiot," said Bombardov, enjoying my fury. "It's got coronary thrombosis, myocarditis and severe neurosis. It spends all day lying on a bed and never sees anybody so naturally it was terrified."

"I agree that the cat's neurotic," I shouted, "but it has the right instincts and it knows all about acting. Even that cat could tell how insincere she was! Don't you see? She was so hopelessly false that the cat was shocked! Anyhow, what was all that pantomime supposed to be about?"

"There'd been a nakladka," explained Bombardov.

"What does that word mean?"

"In theatrical language nakladka means anything that goes wrong on stage. If an actor suddenly fluffs his lines or the curtain doesn't go up on time or . . ."

"I see, I see . . ."

"In the case in question two people were at fault: Augusta Avdeyevna and Nastasya Ivanovna. The first one made the mistake of sending you to Ivan Vasilievich without warning Nastasya Ivanovna that you were coming, and the second by letting Ludmilla Silvestrovna in without first looking to see whether anyone was with Ivan Vasilievich. Although, of course, Augusta Avdeyevna was less to blame, because Nastasya Ivanovna had gone out shopping . . ."

"All right," I said, trying to force myself into a peal of Mephistophelean laughter, "I quite understand! But I still say that your Ludmilla Silvestrovna can't act."

"Oh, come now! People in Moscow say that she acted very well in her time . . ."

"Then people in Moscow are talking rubbish!" I cried. "When she's supposed to be showing sorrow and anguish, her eyes give her away—she's quite obviously furious! She does a little dance and shrieks 'It's an Indian summer' and you can see from her eyes that she's sick with anxiety! When she laughs it sends shivers up your spine as if someone had poured iced soda water over your shirt! She's not an actress!"

"Still, she's been studying Ivan Vasilievich's famous theory of acting for thirty years."

"I don't know anything about his theory, but it obviously hasn't done *her* any good!"

"I suppose you're going to say next that Ivan Vasilievich is no actor?"

"No, of course not. As soon as he showed me how Bakhtin ought to stab himself, I groaned with horror, it was so good. His eyes went dead! He fell on the couch and I was looking at a man who had committed suicide. Judging from that one little scene, just as one can judge a great singer by hearing him sing just one phrase, Ivan Vasilievich must be a wonderful actor. But I simply fail to understand his objections to my play."

"Whatever he says is sensible."

"But that nonsense about the dagger! . . ."

"Look here: you must realize that as soon as you sat down and opened your script he had stopped listening to you. Yes, yes. He was thinking how to cast the play, how to find parts to suit the founder members, how they could stage your play without upsetting the company . . . And then you read out the passage with the shots. I've worked in our theater for ten years and I've been told that only once was a shot ever fired on our stage, in 1901, and it was a frightful disaster. In this play . . . I forget its name . . . the author's famous . . . well, it doesn't matter . . . there were two nervous characters quarreling over an inheritance, quarreling and quarreling until one of them fired a revolver at the other and missed . . . During the ordinary rehearsals the stage manager simulated the shot by clapping his hands, but at the dress rehearsal it was done by letting off a blank cartridge in the wings. Well, Nastasya Ivanovna fainted—she had never heard a shot fired in her life—and Ludmilla Silvestrovna had hysterics. Since then there have been no more shots. The play was changed, the hero didn't shoot but instead he waved a watering can and shouted 'I'll kill you, you scoundrel!' and stamped his foot—all of which, according to Ivan Vasilievich, was the sole cause of the play's success. The author was absolutely furious with the theater management and refused to speak to them for three years, but Ivan Vasilievich was firm . . ."

As that tipsy evening progressed my outbursts weakened and I stopped objecting so noisily to whatever Bombardov said, although I asked plenty more questions. Our mouths were burning after so much salty red caviar and salmon and we slaked our thirst with tea. The room filled with smoke in milky swathes, through the small open windowpane blew a stream of frosty air which only chilled us without freshening the atmosphere.

"Tell me, tell me," I begged in a weak, muffled voice, "in that case, if they won't perform my play, why won't they let me offer it to another theater? I ask you—what use is it to them?"

"Easy! Don't you see? How nice for us if the theater next door puts on a play which could well be a great success! And you ask why! Isn't there a clause in your contract that you won't give it to another theater?"

There leaped to my eyes those rows of sentences all beginning, in fiery green letters, with the words "The Author shall not . . ." and words like "whereas" . . . I remembered all those cunningly phrased paragraphs, the leather-walled office and the faint odor of perfume.

"Curse him!" I screamed.

"Who?"

"Curse him! Gavriil Stepanovich!"

"Vulture!" cried Bombardov, his reddened eyes flashing.

"Yet he looks so gentle and he talks of nothing but his soul! . . ."

"Delusion, delirium, nonsense, lack of powers of observation!" screamed Bombardov. His eyes were burning, his cigarette was burning, smoke was pouring out of his nostrils. "Vulture, condor! There he sits on a cliff top, seeing everything for twenty-five miles around. And the moment a speck appears and moves he takes wing and drops like a stone. A cry of pain, a death rattle . . . and he is climbing heavenward again, his victim in his claws . . ."

"You're a poet, damn you!" I croaked.

"And you," whispered Bombardov, with a thin smile, "are obstinate and hard! Ah, Sergei Leontievich, I predict that you are going to find life difficult . . ."

154

His words transfixed me. I had no idea that I was hard, but then I remembered what Likospastov had said about my wolfish smile. . . .

"So," I said, yawning, "my play won't be put on? It's a total failure?"

Bombardov stared fixedly at me and said with unusual warmth, "You must be prepared for the worst. I won't attempt to deceive you. It won't be put on. Unless a miracle happens . . ."

A grim, misty autumn dawn was breaking. But in spite of the nauseating remains of food scattered over the table, in spite of the mounds of cigarette ends in our saucers, amid all this mess I felt myself inspired by a last wave of emotion and I began to make a speech about the golden horse.

I tried to describe to my audience how the gold had flashed on the horse's mane, how the stage had breathed its cold, secret smell, how the laughter had rippled through the house . . . But that was not my real theme. Knocking over a saucer in my enthusiasm, I tried to convince Bombardov how as soon as I caught sight of the horse I had instinctively grasped the secret of the stage and all its mysteries. How, long ago in childhood perhaps, or perhaps even before I was born I had dreamed of it and longed for it! And now I had arrived in that magic world!

"I'm a stranger in it," I cried, "a stranger in your world—but nothing can stop me! I've arrived—and I shall stay!"

Wheels seemed to turn in my overheated brain, Ludmilla Silvestrovna appeared before me, moaning and waving her lace handkerchief.

"She can't act!" I croaked, almost speechless with fury.

"Look here! You can't . . ."

"Kindly stop contradicting me," I said firmly, "you belong to it but I'm a newcomer, I can still see it all freshly and sharply! I can see through her . . ."

"But . . ."

"And none of your theories are any good! That little snub-nosed man who plays a civil servant, his hands are white, his voice squeaks, but he doesn't need any theory . . . and that one who plays the murderer in black gloves . . . he doesn't need theories—he can *act!*"

"Argunin . . ." I could hear dimly through the blanket of smoke.

"There *are* no theories!" I screamed, drunk with overconfidence and grinding my teeth. At that moment I suddenly noticed an enormous greasy spot on my gray jacket made by a piece of onion that I had dropped. I looked around bewildered. It was no longer night. Bombardov switched off the lamp and in the half-light of dawn everything in the room began to stand out in all its squalor.

The night was gone, eaten up.

CHAPTER FOURTEEN

THE SECRET
MIRACLE WORKERS

THE HUMAN memory is an extraordinary thing. It is no time at all since something was happening yet to try and re-create the event in an orderly sequence proves to be utterly impossible. The links have dropped out of the chain. You remember some of it in a vivid flash, but the rest has crumbled, scattered, leaving nothing in your memory but dust and a shower of rain. Well, dust certainly—but was there really a shower? There must have been because the month after my drunken party with Bombardov was November and of course November is little else but showers alternating with flurries of wet snow. I suppose you know Moscow, don't you? So there is no need for me to describe it. The streets are extremely unpleasant in November. It is even unpleasant indoors; but it's worst of all when you can't even stand being at home. Will somebody please tell me how to get stains out of clothes? I tried everything. It's extraordinary —you dab on benzine and the result is miraculous. The stain fades, fades and disappears. You are delighted, because nothing is more irritating than a stain on your clothes. It's slovenly, dirty and bad for the nerves. You hang up your jacket on a hook, you get up in the morning and—the stain is back where it was, only this time smelling faintly but pervasively of benzine. The same thing happens when you try boiling water, cold tea, eau de cologne. It's diabolical! You get angry, you twitch with annoyance, but it does no good. Obviously anyone who stains his clothes is doomed to walk about with it until it goes of its own accord or until the suit is thrown away. I don't mind about it myself, but I hate the thought of it happening to other people.

So I tried fruitlessly to remove the stain and then, I remember, all my shoelaces broke, I started coughing and turned up daily at the *Gazette*, suffering from the damp and the lack of sunshine. I read books—anything that I happened to pick up. Everybody, for various reasons, deserted me. Likospastov went off to the Caucasus, my friend from whom I stole the revolver was transferred to a job in Leningrad, and Bombardov had to go to the hospital with inflammation of the kidneys. Occasionally I went to visit him, but he didn't feel like talking about the theater. He obviously felt that after the debacle of *Black Snow* it was too delicate a subject to discuss, although he didn't mind discussing his kidney trouble because I could at least console him. So we talked about kidneys and even joked about Professor Klee, although it was somehow not as cheerful as it might have been.

Whenever I saw Bombardov I couldn't help thinking about the theater, but I had enough strength of will not to question him about it. I made a vow not to think about the theater at all, but it was a hopeless resolution. You can't stop yourself thinking.

The theater seemed to have died and gave no sign of life. I heard nothing from them. As I said, I withdrew from human company. I wandered around second-hand bookshops and spent hours squatting in the half-darkness, rummaging among dusty piles of old magazines. In one of them, I remember, I saw a marvelous picture—a triumphal arch . . .

Meanwhile the rainy weather stopped and the frost struck without warning. My attic window was patterned over with frost-flowers and as I sat by the window, breathed on a twenty-kopeck piece and impressed it on the icy surface of the windowpane I realized that to write plays that weren't performed was a waste of time.

Yet in the evenings a waltz filtered through the floor boards, always the same one (someone was learning it by heart) and that waltz brought to life again those strange, disturbing pictures in my imaginary little box. I thought, for instance, that there was an opium den downstairs and I even strung together something which I vaguely thought of as "Act III." It had blue smoke, a woman with an asymmetrical face, a frock-coated opium addict and a man with a lemon face and a squint who was creeping up on him with a sharpened Finnish knife. A blow with the knife, a stream of blood. Rubbish, as you can see! Anyhow, who wants a play with a third act like that!

I never wrote it down. Obviously you're wondering, and I wondered too, why a man who shuts himself up in an attic after suffering a crushing failure and being a melancholic into the bargain (I know I am, don't worry) shouldn't make a second attempt to commit suicide? I confess that my first attempt had produced in me a sort of disgust for this act of violence. True though this was, it wasn't the real reason. There is a time for everything and I would rather not dwell on the subject.

As for the outside world, it was impossible to cut oneself off from it altogether and I couldn't help hearing about it because in the days when I had been getting royalty payments of first fifty and then a hundred rubles from Gavriil Stepanovich I had taken out subscriptions to three theater magazines and the *Moscow Evening News* and these journals arrived more or less regularly. Glancing through *The Stage* I couldn't help reading snippets of news about my theatrical acquaintances. On December fifteenth, for instance, I read: "The well-known writer Ismail Alexandrovich Bondarevsky is finishing a play to be called *The Knives of Montmartre* about emigré life in Paris. The play, we hear, is being offered to the Old Theater."

On the seventeenth I opened a newspaper and read in the latest news: "The distinguished author Y. Agapenov is hard at work on a comedy, *The Brother-in-Law*, which has been commissioned by the Theater of the Cohort of Friends."

On the twenty-second there was a paragraph: "The playwright Klinker, in a talk with our correspondent, announced that he had written a play which he was offering to the Independent Theater. Albert Albertovich tells us that the play is a broad canvas of the Civil War. The play is provisionally entitled *Assault*."

After that on the twenty-third and twenty-fourth similar announcements fell like hail, and on the twenty-sixth the newspaper gave up the whole of its third-page spread to a smudgy picture of a young man with an extraordinarily glum expression, who looked as if he was about to butt somebody with his head. The caption described him as I. S. Trok. Writing a tragedy. Just finishing Act III.

On January second I got really annoyed when I read: "M. Panin, the literary consultant, has called a group of playwrights to the Independent Theater. Theme of the meeting is the writing of a modern play for the Independent Theater." The article was headed "High Time!" and it reproached the Independent Theater with being the only theater never to have put on a single modern play which portrayed our times. "And yet," the newspaper went on, "the Independent, of all the theaters, is the one best fitted to discover a contemporary playwright if only such acknowledged experts as Ivan Vasilievich and Aristarkh Platonovich would set to work to find him." There followed some justified reproaches addressed to playwrights who seemed incapable of producing work that was good enough for the Independent Theater.

I had acquired the habit of talking to myself.

"I beg your pardon," I muttered, pouting with annoyance, "what's that about nobody writing any modern plays? What about the bridge? And the accordion? The blood on the trampled snow?"

A blizzard was whistling outside the window and it seemed that the storm was the storm in the play howling around the bridge, that the accordion was moaning and the sharp crack of shots could be heard in the distance.

My tea was cooling in the glass, a side-whiskered face stared at me from the newspaper page. Beneath it was a quotation from the telegram which Aristarkh Platonovich had sent to Misha Panin's meeting of playwrights: "In Calcutta in body; in spirit with you."

"Oh, the life that's bubbling and seething out there like a millrace," I whispered, yawning, "and here am I, buried alive." Night succeeds night, today fades ceaselessly into tomorrow, time will pass and there will be nothing left but failure. Feeling ill, rubbing my injured knee, I dragged myself to the couch, started to take off my jacket, shivered with cold and wound up my clock.

Many nights passed like that, although I remember them as if they were all one. It was cold in bed. The days have somehow been washed out of my memory—I remember nothing of them.

So my life dragged on until the end of January, when I have a very sharp memory of a dream which I dreamed on the night of the twentieth.

There was a vast chamber in a palace and I was walking up and down in it. Heavy, fat, gilded candles were burning smokily in sconces. I was dressed strangely in long woolen hose—it was not the twentieth century but the fifteenth. As I paced the great hall there was a dagger in my belt. The dream was particularly enjoyable because I clearly had the upper hand thanks to that dagger, of which the courtiers standing in the doorway were visibly frightened. No wine could be as intoxicating as that dagger. Smiling—no, laughing

—in my dream I strode noiselessly toward the doors. The dream was so delightful, in fact, that I went on laughing for some time after I had woken up.

Just then there was a knock at the door and I walked across the room wrapped in a blanket, shuffling my feet in tattered slippers. My neighbor's hand poked itself through the crack and handed me an envelope. On it glittered the golden letters "I.T."

I ripped it open and there, torn diagonally across the page, it lay before me. On the usual paper with the monogram in golden Gothic letters Thomas Strizh had written in his thick, strong hand:

DEAR SERGEI LEONTIEVICH,
    Come to the theater at once! I am starting rehearsals of *Black Snow* tomorrow at twelve noon.
                        Yours,
                                    T. STRIZH

With a stupid grin I sat down on the couch, gazing wildly at the letter and thinking of the dagger, then for some reason of Ludmilla Silvestrovna as I stared at my bare knees.

There was a cheerful and peremptory knock on the door.

"Yes?" I said.

In came Bombardov. Pale, sallow, looking thinner and somehow taller after his illness, his voice, too, changed by it, he said,

"Have you heard? I came especially to tell you."

I let the old blanket drop to the floor and standing in front of him in all my nakedness and misery, I kissed him. The letter fell to the ground.

"How did it happen?" I asked as I bent down to pick it up.

"I have no idea," replied my visitor, "nobody knows and nobody ever will know. I suspect it was arranged by Panin and Strizh, but how they did it, God only knows. It was a superhuman achievement. In fact—it was a miracle."

PART TWO

CHAPTER FIFTEEN

AN INSULATED electric cable lay all over the floor beneath the seats like a thin gray snake that vanished down some invisible hole. It was connected to a tiny lamp on a little table which stood in the center aisle of the seats. The lamp gave exactly enough light to illuminate a sheet of paper and an inkwell on the table. On the paper was a drawing of a snub-nosed face, beside it some still fresh orange peel and an ashtray full of cigarette ends. A faint glitter was reflected from a carafe of water standing just outside the circle of light.

The seats were in such gloom that people coming in from the light would start groping and clutching the backs of the seats until their eyes became used to the dark. The curtains were open and the stage was weakly lit from above through the flies. On stage there was a piece of scenery, its back to the auditorium, marked "Wolves and Sheep—Act II." There was also an armchair, a writing desk and two stools. The armchair was occupied by a workman in a Russian shirt and a jacket and on one of the stools sat a young man wearing a jacket and a pair of trousers. They were belted with a rope from which hung a military saber complete with the special sword knot worn by officers decorated with the St. George's Cross.

The auditorium was stuffy; outside it was a warm day in May.

We were having a break in rehearsal; the actors had gone to have lunch in the buffet and I had stayed behind. The events of the last few months were beginning to tell on me. I felt exhausted and most of the time I wanted to do nothing but sit down and rest for as long as I could. This mood was frequently interrupted by bursts of nervous energy when I felt the urge to rush about, talk, explain, and argue. Now I was having one of my sitting-down spells. Smoke hung in thick layers under the lamp, where the shade sucked it in to expel it upward through the hole in the top.

My thoughts were revolving around one thing—my play. Since the day Strizh had sent me the decisive letter, my life had changed out of all recognition. I was a new man, my room seemed to have altered, although it was the same old room. The people around me had changed and this new man suddenly had a right to live in Moscow: my life had acquired meaning, even importance. I could think of nothing but my play. It monopolized all my time, even when I was asleep. I dreamed of it being performed in the most bizarre settings, dreamed that it had been withdrawn from the repertoire, dreamed of it being a flop and dreamed of it being a hit. In the latter case it was being performed, I remember, on a wooden hillside over which the actors were dotted about like plaster figures, acting with lanterns in their hands and bursting into song every few minutes. I was there too, walking along high, fragile crossbeams as easily as a fly walking on a wall while below me were lime and apple trees, because the play was being performed in a garden full of excited spectators.

My commonest dream of failure was that I was on my way to the dress rehearsal and had forgotten to put on my trousers. I would start off down the street feeling embarrassed but somehow hoping that I could get by without being noticed and even preparing excuses to give to passersby—that I'd just had a bath and that my trousers were hanging up in the wings of the theater. But the further I went the worse it became and there I was rooted to the pavement. I would look for a news vendor, but there wasn't one; I wanted to buy an overcoat, but I hadn't any money. I would finally scuttle into the theater realizing that I was late for the dress rehearsal . . .

"Vanya!" came a faint voice from the stage. "Give us the yellow!"

In the furthest proscenium box a light flared, emitting a funnel-shaped ray which threw a circular patch of yellow light onto the stage. It crept over the floor, grasping the first armchair with its torn upholstery and its chipped gilding, then the disheveled old properties man who was carrying a wooden candlestick. As the end of the rehearsal break drew nearer more and more movement could be heard on stage. The countless rows of canvas screens that hung above the stage suddenly began to move. One of them was hauled upward, instantly uncovering a battery of thousand candle-power bulbs which seared my eyes. Another screen dropped down and was pulled off stage before it reached the floor. Dark shadows began gathering in the wings, the yellow beam was switched off and disappeared as though sucked back into the proscenium box. Somebody started hammering. A man appeared wearing civilian trousers with military spurs and walked clinking around the stage. Then someone kneeled down on the stage floor, cupped his hands to his mouth and shouted into the floor, "O.K., Gnobin!"

Almost soundlessly everything on the stage started to disappear sideways. The prop man and his candlestick were carried away, the armchair and desk glided out. Someone walked on to the moving circle in the opposite direction to its movement, broke into a run and when he was moving at the same speed as the revolve, jumped off. The noise of the machinery grew louder and in place of the previous set there appeared a strange, complex wooden structure made up of crooked, unpainted steps, beams and planks. "Here comes the bridge," I thought and felt the odd, familiar twinge of excitement when it was in position.

"Stop, Gnobin!" came a shout from on stage. "Back a bit!"

The bridge stopped. Then, pouring down a flood of light from gridded reflectors, the great potbellied arc lights were uncovered, covered again, and a crudely painted flat was let down from above and stood diagonally across the stage. "The lodge . . ." I thought, mistaking the layout of the set. It made me nervous to try and imagine how it would all look when instead of a temporary platform knocked together from bits and pieces left over from other plays they would finally build a real bridge. A battery of popeyed spotlights were switched on in the wings, from the foot of the stage poured a live, hot wave of light. "Footlights on . . ."

In the gloom of the auditorium I squinted at the figure who was striding purposefully toward the producer's desk.

"Here comes Romanus. That means things will get going soon . . ." I thought, shielding my eyes with my hand from the light of the lamp. I was right; a few moments later a forked beard loomed over me and the lively eyes of Romanus, the conductor of the orchestra, glittered in the semidarkness. In his buttonhole gleamed the theater's fiftieth anniversary badge with the letters "I.T."

"*Se non è vero, è ben trovato,* or perhaps even better!" began Romanus as usual, his fiery eyes swiveling like the eyes of a wolf in the steppes. Romanus was looking for a victim and, not finding one, sat down beside me.

"Howd' you like it? Eh?" asked Romanus, frowning.

"Oh dear, he's trying to drag me into an argument! . . ." I thought, squirming under the lamplight.

"No, please, tell me your opinion," said Romanus, boring into me with his eye, "I'm sure you find it all so interesting because you're a writer and you must be baffled by all the chaos that goes on here."

"How skillfully he does it . . ." I thought, feeling so uncomfortable that I itched all over.

"Imagine—hitting the leader of the orchestra, and a woman too, in the back with a trombone slide—have you ever heard anything like it?" said Romanus angrily. "Not while I'm conductor! I've been thirty-five years on the stage and I've never seen such a thing. I suppose Strizh thinks that musicians are pigs and they can be shoved into a pigsty. How does that strike you—as a writer?"

I was forced to say something.

"What's happened?"

This was all Romanus was waiting for. In a resonant voice, making sure that he could be heard by the stagehands who had formed an inquisitive group around the footlights, he described how Strizh had crowded the orchestra into a corner of the wings where it was impossible to play for the following reasons: firstly—there wasn't enough room; secondly—it was too dark; thirdly—not a sound could be heard in the auditorium and fourthly—there was nowhere for him to stand so that the musicians could see him.

"Of course there are people," announced Romanus loudly, "who can no more appreciate music than some animals can . . ."

"Oh, go to hell!" I thought.

Romanus' sallies were meeting with success—giggles could be heard coming from the electricians' booth, followed by a head poked out.

"Yes, people like that shouldn't be producing plays, they should be selling kvass outside the Novodevichy cemetery . . ." shouted Romanus in fury.

More giggling.

Apparently Strizh's orders had resulted in chaos. The trombonist had hit Anna Denzhina, the leader, so hard in the back that . . .

". . . when the x-ray is ready we shall see just how serious a matter this is!"

Romanus added that people didn't usually break their ribs in the theater but in the public bar—the place, apparently, where some people had received their artistic training. The joyous red face of an electrician appeared over the top of the booth, his mouth gaping with laughter.

But Romanus insisted that we had not heard the end of this affair. He had told Anna Denzhina what to do. We lived, thank God, in Soviet Russia, where you couldn't just go around breaking trade-union members' ribs. He had told her to make a complaint to the branch committee.

"I'm sure I can see from your expression," went on Romanus, staring at me and trying to draw me into the pool of light, "that you're not fully convinced that our famous branch committee secretary is as well versed in music as Rimski-Korsakov or Schubert!"

"What a bore he is," I thought.

"Oh, really!" I began, trying to sound serious.

"No, let's be frank!" exclaimed Romanus, squeezing my hand. "You're a writer and you must know perfectly well that even if Mitya Malokroshechny had been twenty times branch secretary he couldn't tell an oboe from a cello or a Bach fugue from a fox-trot."

The tenor giggle in the electricians' booth was joined by a hoarse bass. Two heads were now peering delightedly over the top of the booth.

". . . Anton Kaloshin is helping Malokroshechny to improve his knowledge of music. He's the right man to do it because before he came to work in the theater he was in the fire brigade band, where he played the trumpet. If it weren't for Anton," Romanus swore, "a certain producer would have muddled up the overture to *Ruslan and Ludmilla* with a funeral march . . ."

"This man is dangerous," I thought as I looked at Romanus, "really dangerous. There's no way of fighting him!"

". . . If it weren't for Kaloshin the people here would be making musicians play hanging upside down from the ceiling. They think they can get away with it as long as Ivan Vasilievich doesn't come to the theater. Still, they are damn well going to pay Anna Denzhina for her broken rib. It was I, Romanus, who advised her to find out what the trade union's attitude was. It's so outrageous that all I can say is—'Se non è vero, è ben trovato' or perhaps worse!"

Soft footsteps could be heard behind us. Relief was at hand.

It was Andrei Andreyevich. Andrei Andreyevich was the stage manager and he was running the production of Black Snow. He was a fat, fleshy blond man of about forty with the sharp look of a man of great experience. He knew his job well. And an extremely difficult job it was.

As it was now May, Andrei Andreyevich was not wearing his usual dark suit and yellow boots but a blue satin shirt and yellow canvas slippers. He walked toward the desk with his inevitable paper parcel under his arm. Romanus began seething with even greater fury and before Andrei Andreyevich had time to arrange his parcel beside the lamp a scene started.

It began with Romanus saying, "I must categorically protest at acts of violence against the musicians and I request that the incident be entered in the minutes."

"What violence?" asked Andrei Andreyevich in his official voice, with a barely perceptible twitch of one eyebrow.

"If we must produce plays that are more like operas . . ." Romanus began, stopping with an embarrassed choke as he suddenly remembered that the author was sitting beside him, then went on, twisting my side of his face into a smile: ". . . which is a very good thing, because our author fully understands the significance of music in the drama . . . then will you kindly put my orchestra somewhere where they can play!"

"They've been given a place in the wings," said Andrei Andreyevich, pretending that it was a matter of great urgency to open his parcel.

"In the wings? Wouldn't they be better off in the prompter's box? Or sitting in with the prop man?"

"You refused to have the orchestra under the stage."

"Under the stage?" screeched Romanus. "I should damn

well think not! And for your information we're not going to
play in the buffet either!"

"For *your* information I am perfectly aware that we can't
put the orchestra in the buffet," said Andrei Andreyevich, his
other eyebrow starting to twitch.

"You know that," replied Romanus and, quickly making
sure that Strizh was not in the auditorium, he went on: "because you are an old hand and you know something about art,
which is more than can be said about a certain
producer . . ."

"I'm sorry, but you must see the producer about this. He
tested the layout for resonance . . ."

"To test for resonance you need to be equipped by nature
with a suitable apparatus, such as a pair of ears! But some
people seem to have been born . . ."

"I refuse to continue the conversation in this tone," said
Andrei Andreyevich and tied up his parcel again.

"What tone? What tone?" said Romanus in amazement.
"I appeal to this writer, perhaps he will support my view of
the scandalous way musicians are manhandled in this theater!"

"Really, I . . ." was all I could say, gazing dumbstruck at
Andrei Andreyevich.

"No, I'm sorry!" Romanus shouted at Andrei Andreyevich.
"If the stage manager, who is supposed to know the stage
layout like the back of his hand . . ."

"Kindly stop telling me how to do my job," said Andrei
Andreyevich, breaking the string of his parcel.

"I have to, sometimes!" croaked Romanus with a venom-
ous grin.

"I shall have that remark put into the minutes!" said Andrei Andreyevich.

"Please do!"

"Will you kindly stop pestering me? You're disorganizing
the rehearsal!"

"Put that in the minutes too!" screamed Romanus in a
falsetto.

"Kindly stop shouting!"

"You're the one who's shouting!"

"Will you please stop shouting!" rejoined Andrei Andrey-evich, his eyes flashing with temper. He suddenly yelled: "Hey! Lighting! What the hell are you doing up there?" and dashed up the steps onto the stage.

Strizh had come in and was hurrying down the aisle, fol-lowed by the dark silhouettes of the actors. Their entry, I remember, was the signal for the start of a row between Ro-manus and Strizh. Romanus rushed toward him, took him by the arm and said, "Thomas! I know how much you appreci-ate music and it's not your fault, but I must ask you to stop your stage manager from humiliating my musicians!"

"Lighting!" shouted Andrei Andreyevich on the stage, "where's Bobylyov?"

"Gone for his dinner," came a muffled voice in reply.

The actors had gathered in a ring around Strizh and Ro-manus. It was hot, it was May. Hundreds of times, over and over again, these people, their looks dimly enigmatic in the semidarkness above the lampshade, had smeared their faces with paint, transformed themselves, whipped up their emo-tions, worn themselves out. . . . Now the season was well on and they were getting tired; they were nervous, moody and inclined to tease one another with more than a little spite. Romanus looked all set to provide a long and entertaining interruption. Skavronsky, a tall, blue-eyed actor, rubbed his hands joyfully and muttered, "Aha! That's the spirit! You tell him what you really think, Oscar!"

The remark had its effect.

"Will you please not shout at me!" Strizh suddenly roared and thumped the desk with his script.

"Who's shouting now?!" screamed Romanus.

"He's right, by God!" said Skavronsky gaily, egging Ro-manus on. "You're right, Oscar, a rib's more precious than our play," then to Strizh, "Are actors any worse than musi-cians? Think that one over, Oscar!"

"We might as well stop rehearsing," said Yelagin with a yawn, "and have some kvass . . . Will somebody tell me when this quarrel's over?"

• •

The quarrel went on for some time. Shouts could be heard from the circle of lamplight and the smoke spiraled upward, but I had lost interest in their squabble. Wiping the sweat from my forehead I stood by the footlights watching one of the scenery designers, Aurora Gossier, as she walked around the edge of the revolving stage measuring the floor with a yardstick. Her expression was calm, almost sad, her teeth clenched. Whenever she bent over toward the footlights her fair hair shone as though it were on fire, and then dimmed to an ashen color as she turned away. I reminded myself that all this agonizingly slow procedure would come to an end . . .

Meanwhile the quarrel had finished.

"Come on, now, come on!" shouted Strizh. "We're wasting time!"

Patrikeyev, Vladychensky and Skavronsky were already wandering about the stage among the prop men. Romanus, too, had followed them onto the stage. His appearance soon produced its effect. He walked up to Vladychensky and asked him anxiously whether he didn't think that Patrikeyev rather overdid the clowning, so that the audience was bound to burst out laughing at the very moment when Vladychensky was speaking his big line, "And what's to become of me? I'm alone and I'm ill . . ."

Vladychensky went as pale as death and a minute later the actors, the stagehands and the prop men were all standing in a row by the footlights listening to a swearing match between the two long-standing enemies, Vladychensky and Patrikeyev. Vladychensky, an athletically-built man, naturally pale and now even paler with anger, clenching his fists and trying his best to make his powerful voice sound terrifying, was saying, without looking at Patrikeyev, "I'm very concerned about this whole problem. It's high time we did something about these circus artistes who play for cheap laughs the whole time and give this theater a bad name!"

Patrikeyev, a comedy actor who played juvenile leads of all kinds and who off stage, although fat, was an unusually adroit and adaptable man, tried to look simultaneously scornful and furious, the result being that his eyes registered distress and his face physical pain. In a husky voice he replied, "I think you're forgetting—I am an actor of the Independent Theater and not a cinema extra like you!"

Romanus stood in the wings, beaming with satisfaction. The noise of the two men quarreling completely drowned Strizh's voice as he shouted from his seat, "Stop this minute, will you? Andrei Andreyevich! Send out the alarm call for Stroyev! Where is he? He's holding up my timetable!"

With a practiced hand Andrei Andreyevich pressed a button on the stage manager's control panel and from far away, from the buffet, from the foyer, came the piercing, urgent ringing of a bell. Stroyev, who had been gossiping with Toropetzkaya in the changing room, came leaping downstairs and onto the stage, which he reached through the scenery dock without crossing the auditorium, and with a faint jingle from the spurs strapped over his civilian trousers he took up a position in the wings near the footlights, skillfully giving the impression that he had been there all the time.

"Where's Stroyev?" roared Strizh. "Ring for him! You two —stop quarreling, damn you!"

"I'll ring again," said Andrei Andreyevich. He turned and caught sight of Stroyev. "I've just given you an alarm call!" said Andrei Andreyevich sternly, and immediately the bells throughout the theater ceased.

"Me?" replied Stroyev. "Why me? I've been here for at least ten minutes, if not a quarter of an hour . . . *Mamma mia!*" He cleared his throat.

Andrei Andreyevich took a deep breath, said nothing but gave Stroyev a meaning look. Instead he used the breath to shout, "Everybody not in this scene—off stage! We're starting!"

Everything stopped. The prop men walked off, the actors took up their positions. In the wings Romanus congratulated Patrikeyev for standing up so manfully to Vladychensky, who had been asking for trouble for a long time.

CHAPTER SIXTEEN

A
SUCCESSFUL MARRIAGE

JUNE was even hotter than May.

I remember that, but the memory of everything else is strangely blurred. However, a few snatches remain, such as the arrival of Drykin's coach at the theater steps, with Drykin himself sitting on the box in a quilted blue caftan, and the astonished faces of the automobile drivers as they dodged Drykin's ancient vehicle.

Then I remember a big hall in which actors were sitting about on an untidy litter of chairs. Behind a table spread with a cloth were Ivan Vasilievich, Thomas Strizh and myself.

During this period I got to know Ivan Vasilievich more closely and I may say that I recollect the time as one of considerable strain. This was a result of my desperate efforts to make a good impression on Ivan Vasilievich.

Every other day I gave my suit to Dusya to press, for which I paid her regularly.

Under an archway I found a flimsy little draper's stall, apparently built of cardboard and kept by a fat man with two diamond rings on his fingers from whom I bought twenty starched collars. Every day before going to the theater I would put on a clean one. In addition I bought, not at the stall but in the state department store, six shirts: four white ones, one with lilac stripes, one with a blue check and four assorted neckties. From a man who used to sit, hatless whatever the weather, at a street-corner stall in the center of Moscow, I bought two tins of yellow shoe polish and every morning I borrowed a brush from Dusya and cleaned my yellow shoes, polishing them with the hem of my dressing gown.

This enormous extra expenditure drove me to write a short story in two nights, which I entitled *The Flea*, and with this story in my pocket I spent my spare time from rehearsals trailing around the offices of weekly magazines trying to sell it. I began with the editor of the *Shipping Gazette*, who liked the story but refused to print it on the perfectly reasonable grounds that it had nothing whatever to do with marine transport. It would be too long and boring to describe all the editorial offices that I visited and why they all turned me down. I can only recall that everywhere I went I got a hostile reception. I particularly remember some fat man with a pince-nez who not only flatly refused to print my story but gave me a stiff lecture into the bargain.

"Your story gives the impression that you are addressing the reader with a sly wink," said the fat man, staring at me with disgust.

I must defend myself—the fat man was wrong. There was no trace of a sly wink in my story but (I can admit it now) the story was boring, inept and complete proof that I utterly lacked any talent for writing short stories. In spite of that a miracle happened. After I had offered it all over Moscow I unexpectedly sold it to a man with an enormous birthmark in his cheek in an office on, if I remember correctly, the fifth floor. Having collected my money and closed the fearful gap

in my budget I went back to the theater, which I now needed
as much as an addict needs his morphine.

I must confess with a heavy heart that all my efforts were
in vain and even, to my horror, produced the opposite effect.
Every day Ivan Vasilievich liked me less and less. Don't imagine that I based all my calculations on nothing but a pair of
gleaming yellow shoes. Oh no! It was an operation of considerable skill, cunning and complexity, which included tech-
niques such as speaking in a deep, soft, penetrating voice. The
voice was combined with a look which radiated honesty, sin-
cerity and directness and a light smile of utterly unservile
simplicity. My hair was immaculately combed, I shaved so
carefully that even when I rubbed the bottom of the shaving
brush handle over my cheek there was not a sign of stubble.
The opinions I gave were brief, intelligent and staggeringly
well-informed—and none of it did the slightest good. At first
Ivan Vasilievich smiled whenever he met me, then his smiles
grew increasingly rare and in the end he stopped smiling altogether.

I started holding rehearsals at night. I would take a small
mirror, sit in front of it, watch my reflection and speak, "Ivan
Vasilievich! Look, this is the point: in my opinion we can't
use a dagger because . . ."
It was highly successful. A modest, dignified smile hovered
over my lips, my eyes stared frankly and intelligently into the
mirror, my brow was smooth, my parting lay like a white
thread straight across my black hair. It couldn't fail to produce results—and yet the actual effect was disastrous. I became exhausted, grew thinner and slightly relaxed my efforts
at sartorial perfection. I even wore the same collar two days
running.
One night I decided to put myself to the test and recited
my monologue without looking into the mirror, then squinted
furtively into the glass to check upon myself and was appalled. From the mirror a face stared at me with frowning
brow, bared teeth and eyes which betrayed a mixture of

anxiety and low cunning. I clutched my head, realizing that the mirror had cheated me and I threw it on the ground. As it smashed, a triangular piece fell out. They say that breaking a mirror means bad luck. What can one say of a lunatic who breaks his own mirror?

"You fool, you fool!" I cried, my wails sounding like the hooting of an owl. "I was all right as long as I was staring at myself in the mirror but the moment I look away all my self-control vanishes and my face shows exactly what I'm really thinking and . . . oh God, oh God!"

I have no doubt that if anyone ever finds these jottings of mine, they will not make a particularly good impression on their reader. He's bound to see me as a sly, two-faced poseur trying for his own mercenary ends to impress Ivan Vasilie-vich. Do not, however, judge me too hastily. I'll tell you why I felt the need to be so devious.

Ivan Vasilievich was obstinately insisting on cutting out the scene where Bakhtin (or Bakhteyev, as Ivan Vasilievich preferred it) shot himself, where the moon shone and the sound of an accordion was heard, whereas I saw that without that scene the play was dead. And it *had* to come to life, because I knew that there was truth in the play. Ivan Vasilie-vich's motives were, of course, all too clear and they were obviously irrelevant, but I had been studying him carefully since our first meeting and I realized that he was totally in-vulnerable to attack. I had only one method left—to try and get him to listen to me. For that he naturally had to like me. Hence my efforts with the mirror. I was trying to save that shot: I wanted people to hear the poignant music of the ac-cordion on that bridge, to see the blood spreading on the moonlit snow. I wanted them to see that patch of black snow. That was all.

Once again the owl hooted, "You fool! Don't you see? How can you make somebody like you when you don't like him? Do you really imagine you can fool a man like that? You resent him, and yet you're trying to make him see your point of view! You'll never succeed, however much you pull faces in front of a mirror."

And I didn't like Ivan Vasilievich. Nor did I like his aunt Nastasya Ivanovna and I loathed Ludmilla Silvestrovna. People can sense these things.

The arrival of Drykin's cab meant that Ivan Vasilievich was coming to the theater for a rehearsal of *Black Snow*. Every day at noon Pakin came galloping into the darkened stalls, grinning with fear and carrying a pair of galoshes. Behind him came Augusta Avdeyevna with a tartan rug over her arm, behind her Ludmilla Silvestrovna with her notebook and lace handkerchief.

Once in the auditorium Ivan Vasilievich put on his galoshes and sat down at the producer's desk, Augusta Avdeyevna draped the rug around his shoulders and the rehearsal would begin.

During rehearsal Ludmilla Silvestrovna would choose a perch not far from the producer's desk and make notes in her exercise book, occasionally uttering muffled cries of ecstasy.

I must now make a confession. The reason for my hostility, which I tried by such idiotic means to conceal, had nothing to do with his rug or his galoshes, or even with Ludmilla Silvestrovna, but simply with the fact that Ivan Vasilievich, after fifty-five years of work as a producer, had invented the famous "method"—universally regarded as a creation of genius—which prescribes how an actor should prepare himself to play a part.

I don't doubt for a moment that the method really is a work of genius, but the practical application of it reduced me to despair. I swear that if I were to bring a layman into a rehearsal he would be amazed.

In my play Patrikeyev was playing the part of a minor official in love with a woman who did not love him. The part was funny, and Patrikeyev played it with great comic effect and increasing mastery. He was so good that I began to feel that he wasn't Patrikeyev at all but the man I had invented, and that Patrikeyev himself had a separate existence.

As soon as the horse-drawn cab had arrived at the theater

and Ivan Vasilievich had been enrobed in his tartan, the rehearsal started by working on one of Patrikeyev's scenes.

"Very well, let us commence," said Ivan Vasilievich.

A reverential hush spread over the auditorium and the nervous Patrikeyev (his nervousness showed in his eyes, which seemed on the verge of tears) played the scene in which he declared his love for the girl.

"That," said Ivan Vasilievich, eyes flashing through his lorgnette, "is no good at all."

I groaned inwardly and something turned over in my stomach. I couldn't imagine how anyone could possibly play the scene an atom better than Patrikeyev had played it. "And if he succeeds in improving it," I thought, as I looked respectfully at Ivan Vasilievich, "I'll admit that he really is a genius."

"No good at all," repeated Ivan Vasilievich. "It's like an amateur revue sketch. What are his feelings for that woman?"

"He loves her, Ivan Vasilievich! Oh, how he loves her!" cried Thomas Strizh.

"I see," replied Ivan Vasilievich and turned back to Patrikeyev. "Have you ever thought what passionate love is like?"

For an answer Patrikeyev mumbled something from the stage, but it it was inaudible.

"Passionate love," went on Ivan Vasilievich, "is expressed by the man being prepared to do anything for his beloved." And with that he ordered, "Bring on a bicycle!"

Ivan Vasilievich's order delighted Strizh, who shouted in an urgent voice: "Hey, props! Bicycle!"

The prop man wheeled on to the stage an ancient bicycle with a peeling frame. Patrikeyev gave it a tearful look.

"Everything the lover does he does for his beloved," said Ivan Vasilievich. "He eats for her, drinks for her, walks and rides for her . . ."

My heart pounding with interest and curiosity, I glanced at Ludmilla Silvestrovna's square-ruled exercise book and saw her writing in a childish hand: "The lover does everything for his beloved . . ."

"Now please take a ride on that bicycle for your beloved," ordered Ivan Vasilievich and ate a mint lozenge.

I stared at the stage. Patrikeyev clambered onto the machine, the actress playing the beloved sat down in a chair, clutching an enormous patent-leather handbag. Patrikeyev pedaled off and described a wobbly course around the chair, squinting with one eye at the prompter's box, which he was afraid of hitting, and with the other eye at the actress. Smiles broke out all over the auditorium.

"Quite wrong," said Ivan Vasilievich when Patrikeyev had stopped. "Why were you staring at the prompter? Were you riding for him?"

Patrikeyev rode around again, this time squinting with both eyes at the actress. He failed to turn the corner and pedaled off into the wings. When they had brought him back, pushing the bicycle by the handlebars, Ivan Vasilievich was still not satisfied and Patrikeyev set off for a third time, his head turned toward the actress.

"Terrible!" said Ivan Vasilievich bitterly. "Your muscles are all tense, you lack confidence in yourself. Relax your muscles, let them go! Your head was unnatural, you don't trust it."

Patrikeyev rode off again, head down and staring at the girl from under his eyebrows.

"Empty—you were riding emptily, instead of being filled with your beloved."

So Patrikeyev set off once more. He circled around once, leaning over sideways and staring longingly at his paramour. Steering with one hand he made a sharp turn, bore down on the actress and smeared her skirt with his dirty front tire. The girl gave a frightened shriek, which was echoed by a shriek from Ludmilla Silvestrovna in the seats. Having made sure that the actress had not been wounded and was not in need of medical assistance, Ivan Vasilievich, reassured that nothing terrible had happened, sent Patrikeyev cycling off again. He went on circling around until Ivan Vasilievich finally inquired whether he was tired. Patrikeyev said he wasn't, but Ivan Vasilievich said that he could see that Patrikcyev was tired and the actor was allowed a break.

His place was taken by a group of guests. I went out to the buffet for a smoke and when I returned I saw that the actress' handbag was lying on the ground and she herself was sitting on her hands as were the three male and one female characters. The latter was Veshnyakova, who had been mentioned in the letter from India. They were all trying to speak the lines according to the script, but they could make no progress because Ivan Vasilievich stopped them every time an actor said something and explained why it was wrong. The task of the guests and of Patrikeyev's sweetheart—the heroine of the play—was made doubly hard by being forbidden to use their hands. Noticing my astonishment, Strizh explained to me in a whisper that Ivan Vasilievich had deprived them of their hands on purpose, in order to force them to make sense of the dialogue unaided by gesture.

Surfeited with new and strange impressions I returned home from the rehearsal, saying to myself, "It's all quite extraordinary, but only because I'm a layman. Every art has its rules, its methods and its secrets. A savage might think it most odd for people to clean their teeth with a brush loaded with chalky paste. It must seem just as strange to the uninitiated that before operating a surgeon does a number of incomprehensible things to the patient, such as taking blood tests and so on . . ."

Most of all I longed to see the result of the bicycle act at the next rehearsal, to discover whether Patrikeyev would succeed in cycling "for her." Next day, however, not a word was said about the bicycle, although I saw several more no less amazing tricks. Patrikeyev had to offer a bouquet to his sweetheart. This began at noon and lasted until four o'clock.

Not only Patrikeyev was made to offer the bouquet but all the other actors in turn, including Yelagin who was playing the general and even Adalbert who had the part of the chief of the bandit gang. This I found particularly odd, but Strizh reassured me by explaining that as usual Ivan Vasilievich was showing great wisdom in teaching a point of stage technique to several actors at once. Ivan Vasilievich accompanied the lesson with some interesting and instructive stories about how one should offer a lady a bouquet and the various ways in which other actors had done it. From this I learned that the greatest masters of this particular art had been the famous Komarovsky-Bioncourt (at this point Ludmilla ruined the rehearsal by shrieking, "Ah, yes, Ivan Vasilievich, he was unforgettable!") and an Italian baritone whom Ivan Vasilievich had once met in Milan in 1889.

Without having known that baritone I must say that Ivan Vasilievich himself was by far the best at offering a bouquet. Full of enthusiasm he went on stage and showed us thirteen times how it should be done. I began to believe that Ivan Vasilievich really was an actor of genius.

Next day I was late for rehearsal and when I arrived I saw sitting side by side on the stage Olga Sergeyevna (the actress playing the heroine) and Veshnyakova, Yelagin, Vladychensky, Adalbert and several others unknown to me and at Ivan Vasilievich's command of "One, two, three" they all started taking invisible wallets out of their pockets, counting invisible money and putting the money back.

When this étude was over (the reason for it was that Patrikeyev had to count some money in that scene) another one began. Andrei Andreyevich called a mass of people onto the stage and sat them down on chairs. With invisible pens, on invisible tables they began writing letters on invisible paper and sealing them up. The trick was that the letter was supposed to be a love letter. This étude was spoiled by a slight misunderstanding, because one of the prop men was included in the writing class by mistake. Not yet knowing many of the new company members by sight, Ivan Vasilievich rounded up a mop-headed young man, who happened to be loitering on the edge of the stage, to join in writing the imaginary letter.

"And what about you," Ivan Vasilievich shouted at him, "are you going to send a telegram instead?"

The man sat down on a chair and joined the others in writing on air and spitting on his fingers. To my eyes he did it no worse than the others, although he wore an embarrassed smile and was rather red in the face, which made Ivan Vasilievich shout at him: "Who's that humorist on the end of the row? Does he think he's training for the circus? Why isn't he taking it seriously? What's his name?"

"He's a prop man, Ivan Vasilievich!" groaned Strizh. The master was silent and the prop man was allowed to go.

The days passed in unceasing labor. I saw a great deal. I saw, for instance, a crowd of actors headed by Ludmilla Silvestrovna (who incidentally had no part in the play) charge shrieking about the stage and then lean out of invisible windows. The reason was that in the same scene with the bouquet and the letter business, my heroine had to run to the window from which she caught sight of the distant glow of a fire. This provided the excuse for a protracted étude, which was blown up to incredible proportions and which reduced me, I must confess, to a state of near despair.

Ivan Vasilievich ordered everybody to act out the scene from their own imagination. Part of his theory was the idea that at rehearsal the script should be completely disregarded and the play's characters had to be created impromptu. As a result, every actor, as he rushed to the window, shouted out whatever he felt like saying. The commonest exclamation was "Oh, my God, my God!" Adalbert exclaimed, "What's on fire? Where is it?" Others shouted, "Help! Water! Eliseyev's on fire! Save the children! There's an explosion! Call the fire brigade! We'll all be burned to death!"

Over all this hubbub soared the piercing voice of Ludmilla Silvestrovna, who was yelling the most utter nonsense, "Oh, my God! God almighty! What will become of my trunks?! And my diamonds, my diamonds!"

Darkening like a thundercloud I watched Ludmilla Silvestrovna wringing her hands and thought how the heroine of my play had only one short line to say: "Look—there's a fire . . ." and said it beautifully. I was bored to death by having to watch Ludmilla Silvestrovna emote all over the stage. Her wild shrieks about trunks and diamonds had nothing whatever to do with the play and she irritated me so violently that my face began to twitch.

By the end of the third week of rehearsals under Ivan Vasilievich I was in real despair. There were three reasons for this. Firstly, I had done a little simple arithmetic and the result appalled me: we had spent three weeks rehearsing the same scene. The play contained seven scenes. If we were going to take three weeks over every scene . . .

"Oh, Lord!" I whispered as I tossed sleeplessly on my couch "three times seven . . . is twenty-one weeks which is . . . five . . . yes, five . . . maybe even six months! When on earth is my play going to open?! The season finishes in a week's time and then there won't be any more rehearsals until September! Godfathers! September, October, November . . ." The night turned into dawn. My window was open, but the morning was as warm and airless as the night. I arrived at the rehearsal with migraine, looking yellow and drawn.

My second worry was even more serious. I can only divulge my awful secret to this notebook, I had doubts about Ivan Vasilievich's "theory." Yes, it sounds terrible, but it's true. Sinister doubts had begun to creep into my mind as early as the end of the first week. By the end of the second I realized that the famous theory was utterly wrong for my play. Far from getting any better at proffering his bouquet, writing a letter or declaring his love, Patrikeyev got more and more awkward, dry and completely un-funny. Worst of all, he suddenly caught a cold.

When I told this sad news to Bombardov, he laughed and said, "His cold won't last long. He's feeling better already and yesterday he was playing billiards in the club. As soon as they finish rehearsing that scene his cold will get better. You wait and see—the others will soon start getting colds too. My guess is that Yelagin will be the first."

"Oh, hell!" I exclaimed, beginning to understand.

Bombardov's prediction came true. A day later Yelagin was absent from rehearsal and against his name Andrei Andreyevich wrote in the minutes: "Excused rehearsal due to a cold." Adalbert, too, was struck down and after him Veshnyakova. I ground my teeth and added another month to my multiplication sum to allow for colds, but I couldn't blame Adalbert or Patrikeyev. After all, why should a bandit chief waste his time shrieking about a nonexistent fire that took place in Scene IV when he wanted to be practicing his banditry in Scene III and Scene V?

So while Patrikeyev wielded his cue in a long game of American billiards, Adalbert was rehearsing Schiller's *Die Räuber* at a club in Krasnaya Presnya where he ran the amateur theatrical group.

I was convinced that the "theory" was not only unsuited to my play but actually harmful. The quarrel between two of the characters in Scene IV included the sentence: "I challenge you to a duel!" Time and again I swore that I would cut off my hand for having written that fatal line. As soon as it was spoken at rehearsal, Ivan Vasilievich became very excited and ordered rapiers to be brought on. I turned pale and stared in fury as Vladychensky and Blagosvetlov clinked blades, trembling in case one of them might stab the other in the eye.

Meanwhile Ivan Vasilievich told a story about the day when Komorovsky-Bioncourt had fought a saber duel with the son of the mayor of Moscow. I didn't give a damn for the mayor of Moscow's wretched son, but I was irritated beyond endurance by Ivan Vasilievich's efforts to force me into rewriting the duel scene as a fight with sabers. I treated the idea as a bad joke, but imagine my feelings when the treacherous Strizh said that he wanted the new duel scene "sketched out" within a week. I started arguing, but Strizh was adamant. What finally reduced me to utter fury was the entry in his producer's notebook: "Duel with swords."

My relations with Strizh grew increasingly strained.

Angry, bewildered, I turned restlessly from side to side in bed. I felt humiliated.

"I bet they didn't write duels into Ostrovsky's plays," I grumbled, "and I bet they didn't let Ludmilla Silvestrovna scream away about trunks either!"

Yet although this made me resent Ostrovsky as though he

were still alive, my quarrel was a personal one and only concerned my play. A more powerful influence was at work in me: consumed with love for the Independent Theater, pinned to it like a beetle to a piece of cork, nothing could keep me from seeing every performance . . .

AFTERWORD

I SHOULD have warned the reader that I had nothing whatever to do with the aforegoing jottings, which reached me under very odd and distressing circumstances.

On the very day that Sergei Leontievich Maxudov committed suicide, an event which took place in Kiev in the spring of last year, I received a bulging wrapper and a letter which had been dispatched by the suicide just before his death. In the wrapper were his notes—the aforegoing—and a most extraordinary letter, in which Sergei Leontievich announced that on leaving this life he was presenting me with his notes in order that I—his only friend—should sort them out, head them with my own name and publish them.

A strange wish, but the will of a dying man . . .

For a year I searched for relatives or close friends of Sergei Leontievich, but in vain. He had not been lying in his farewell letter; he had no one left in this world. I therefore accepted his gift.

Now for my second point: Maxudov had no connection whatsoever with playwriting or with the theater in his life, and he remained what he always had been—a minor employee of the newspaper the *Shipping Gazette*; he had only once ventured into literature and even then unsuccessfully—his novel was never published. Maxudov's notes, therefore, are the fruit of his imagination, an imagination which was, alas, morbid. Sergei Leontievich suffered from a disease with a very unpleasant name—melancholia. Knowing Moscow theatrical life as well as I do, I am prepared to swear that the theaters and the people described in the late author's works do not exist and never have existed.

Finally, my third and last point: my work on these notes consisted of dividing them into chapters and then in erasing the epigraph, which seemed to me pretentious, unnecessary and disagreeable. The epigraph read: "To someone, who knows why . . ." Apart from that I merely corrected the punctuation where it was inadequate.

I did not touch Sergei Leontievich's style, although it is clearly slovenly. But what can you expect from a man who, two days after putting the last full stop to his notes, threw himself headlong from the Chain Bridge?